dragon's tear

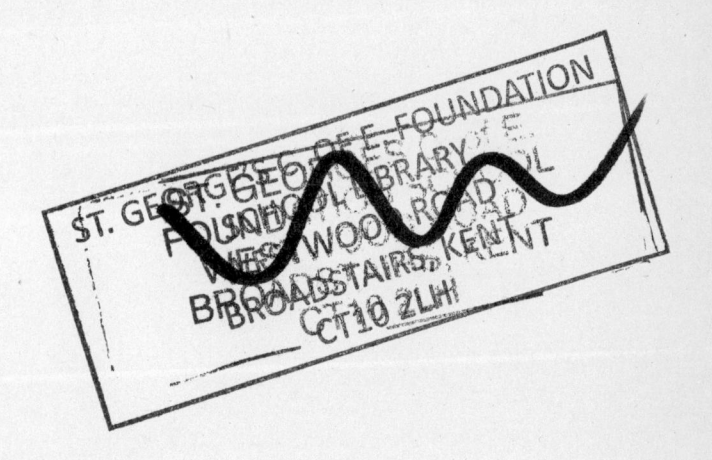

Takeaways

Are You Listening?, Lydia Sturton
Newbjorn, Kathryn England
Blue Fin, Colin Thiele
The Changeling, Gail Merritt
Chickenpox, Yuk!, Josie Montano
The Dog King, Paul Collins
Dragon's Tear, Sue Lawson
Fake ID, Hazel Edwards
Fries, Ken Catran
Get a Life!, Krista Bell
The Grandfather Clock, Anthony Hill
The Great Ferret Race, Paul Collins
It's Time, Cassandra Klein, Karen R. Brooks
Jodie's Journey, Colin Thiele
The Keeper, Rosanne Hawke
Landslide, Colin Thiele
The Lyrebird's Tail, Susan Robinson
Monstered, Bernie Monagle
Mystery at Devon House, Cory Daniells
Ned's Kang-u-roo, Vashti Farrer
NIPS XI, Ruth Starke
No Regrets, Krista Bell
Pop Starlets, Josie Montano
Read My Mind!, Krista Bell
The Rescue of Princess Athena, Kathryn England
Sailmaker, Rosanne Hawke
Saving Saddler Street, Ruth Starke
The Sea Caves, Colin Thiele
Seashores and Shadows, Colin Thiele
Space Games, Mike Carter
Spy Babies, Ian Bone
Swan Song, Colin Thiele
Timmy, Colin Thiele
Twice upon a Time, John Pinkney
Wendy's Whale, Colin Thiele
The Worst Year of My Life, Katherine Goode

dragon's tear

Sue Lawson

Lothian
BOOKS

To Bruce and Courtney, the lights of my life

Acknowledgements

Special thanks to my friend Eve Martyn (Eve Old) for her hours of toil and sage advice, and to John Marsden for his generosity and foresight in conducting the Tye Estate Writers' Conferences.

Thomas C. Lothian Pty Ltd
132 Albert Road, South Melbourne, Victoria 3205
www.lothian.com.au

Copyright © Sue Lawson 2002
First published 2002
Reprinted 2002

All rights reserved. No part of this publication may be reproduced, stored in a retrieval system or transmitted in any form by any means without the prior permission of the copyright owner. Enquiries should be made to the publisher.

National Library of Australia
Cataloguing-in-publication data:

Lawson, Sue, 1969- .
Dragon's tear.

For children.
ISBN 0 7344 0326 7 (pbk.).

1. Friendship - Juvenile fiction.
2. Dragons - Juvenile fiction. I. Title.

A823.4

Cover design by Michelle Macintosh
Cover and text illustrations by Marc McBride
Book design by Paulene Meyer
Printed in Australia by Griffin Press

one

It's a good idea to keep out of my mother's way when she's angry — hide under the bed, hide behind the couch or leave the house — just get out of her way.

Before we moved to Wilton, Mum was pretty normal. She'd get angry about weird things, like leaving the lid off the toothpaste or getting margarine in the Vegemite jar, but she used to laugh too. Then Dad bought The Corner Store and moved us to Wilton, two and a half hours from the city and three hours from Beldare. He didn't ask any of us what we thought, not even Mum. And that's when she started acting like a puffer fish. One minute she'd be darting around this way and that, when — *poof* — she seemed to swell to twice her tiny size, her eyes would bulge, and you could almost see the spikes burst out of her pale skin. And her voice — I reckon if an angry shark could talk, it would sound just the same and just as loud. Mum always rolled her eyes a little before an attack, so as soon as I saw a flicker in those black-rimmed eyes, I was out of there.

I missed the signs this morning and blundered straight into an attack. Mum puffed up in front of the back door — the door to freedom. The only other escape route was through the shop, but seeing as Mrs Johnston had Dad pinned down by the ice-cream freezer, I was staying clear of there.

Dad says we should be nice to Mrs Johnston. He says her husband died years ago and she's been alone ever since. No wonder! With a voice like a milkshake machine and horrible clown-red lipstick, who'd want to marry her? She wears her lipstick on her lips, chin, and the bumpy bit under her nose. It's even on top of her dog's head. Poor thing. My brother Justin and I worked out she kisses the top of its head, but that doesn't make us rocket scientists. Justin and I call her Pucker. Dad calls us disrespectful.

So it was either Pucker and the latest adventures of Midge the Lipstick Terrier, or an attack from my puffer-fish mother. I decided to go toe-to-fin with the puffer fish.

'I wonder if it's sunny in Seal Point, too?' The venetian blinds snapped and swayed as I forced them apart and peered at the clear sky. I'd decided to try that suggestive stuff you read about in magazines. Maybe if I talked about Seal Point enough I could get Mum to change her mind.

Mum sighed. 'Cam, please, we've already discussed this.'

'I know. I was just thinking aloud.' I cleared my throat. 'The kids at school reckon it's always sunny at Seal Point.'

'They're wrong, Cameron. The weather's not much different from here.'

'But we don't know that for sure. If we went and stayed, just for a weekend —'

'Cameron, how many times do I have to tell you?' Mum's eyes bulged and glittered. 'We will not be going to Seal Point. Not for a weekend, not even for a day.'

'But, Mum, everyone is going to Seal Point. Can't we go just for a couple of days?'

'We can't afford the time or the money.' Mum rubbed her eyes, sighed and went back to stabbing the order book with her red pen, perfect pink nails clicking with each stab.

'Seal Point is only forty minutes —'

'Cameron!' The shark's voice. I hoped Dad and Pucker were still beside the ice-cream fridge. It chugged and spluttered enough to drown out even Mum's shark voice. 'Stop talking about Seal Point. Do something useful — go help your dad in the shop.' She paused and fixed me with her bulging eyes. 'And don't eat anything.' The sea-snake-venom voice. She kept this voice for when she was in a seriously bad mood.

I squeezed the tennis ball in my left hand,

and, with my right, held my stomach, trying to protect it from the attack.

I was on dangerous ground, but I had to try again. Going to Seal Point would make my life at school next year. Before the summer holidays, all the kids in my grade, except Tim Franklin, had planned swimming, snorkeling and surfing adventures. I'd sat and listened, kicking dust with my scuffed boot, pretending I didn't care. But I did. Matt and Josh got sick of planning and started giving Tim and me heaps because we weren't going. I couldn't believe how Tim stood up to them. I tried, but I couldn't. If my family went to Seal Point, even for a weekend, Matt and Josh would see I was as cool as they were and once they saw me swim and surf, they'd be desperate to be my friends.

'I've saved forty-three dollars, Mum. We could use that.'

Mum's red pen whizzed past my ear, clattered into the wall and landed in the empty fruit bowl. Her chair crashed behind her as she stood, swelling to bursting point.

'Since your father made us come to this … place,' she spat out the word and flipped her hand at the grey room, 'we have no money and no life. All I do is fill out numbers in this stupid b-b-book!' She banged the table with her open hand so hard the papers and order pads did a little skip, like lambs playing in a paddock. 'And all you do is whinge about Seal Point. Why don't you try helping for a change?' Her eyes narrowed so much it was a wonder she could see. 'You're just like your father. Thank goodness Justin is more like me. He helps out. He's earned a holiday at Seal Point.'

I gasped. My knees buckled like they did when Matt punched me in the guts till I gave him my footy cards.

She wouldn't let Justin go to Seal Point to snorkel and surf with the cool kids while I stayed home and talked to lipstick-stained terriers — would she? Surely I'd misunderstood.

'Is Justin going to Seal Point?' My lips moved but my jaw stayed clamped shut.

'The Davidsons asked him to stay with them. He and Michael are such good friends.' This was a new voice — like one of those mums in the old TV shows like the Brady Bunch. She smiled — with her lips. 'Why don't you ask one of your friends if you could stay with them?' She reached for her seat, pulled it back under her and folded her hands on the table.

My eyes stung and a lump blocked my throat. She sure knew how to hurt a person. She knew I had no friends in Wilton. She knew I was lonely. I'd told her just last week. I'd wanted to cry, I really did, but I didn't. I hadn't cried since my bitser, Bunty, chased one of Justin's stupid cricket balls out the front gate onto Beldare Road. The 12.50 bus to the city flattened my dog and the cricket ball. I thought my chest would burst like a water bomb — splat — all over the place.

Being lonely hurt nearly as much as losing Bunty. I thought Mum understood all that. My toes curled, bunching my Nikes. My free hand became an iron fist, the other squeezed the tennis ball till I thought it'd pop. 'Remember, Mum? I haven't got any friends.'

Mum reached for a pen and, keeping her eyes

fixed on the table, commented, 'If you were more like your brother, you'd —'

It was my turn to puff up. My vision blurred and became misty red. Anger gathered in my fists and toes, crackling at Mum like a bushfire. I grabbed the order book with my free hand and flung it. It thudded against the wall behind her head. I sprinted out the back door and jumped on my bike, screaming over my shoulder as I pedalled away. 'I hate you and that dork Justin.'

two

I leant on my handlebars and looked around me. I'd stopped in a patch of trees on the hill overlooking Lake Warrong.

My teacher, Mrs Samson, told us Wilton had been settled on the shores of Lake Warrong over 150 years ago. Back then the lake had been ringed by bushland and empty rolling hills. Native trees and bushland still grew in some spots, and were quite thick here on the north side, but now farms, factories and houses crowded its banks. Mrs

Samson told us the water had been crystal clear and brimming with life. Now it was muddy and littered with rubbish.

I stared down at the cool, calm lake. Rippling waves lapped the shore, leaving small wriggling lines of creamy foam. A cool breeze skipped across the lake's surface, darted through the bullrushes and raced up the hill, whispering secrets to the gum leaves. Water birds puddled in the mud and squabbled with bossy black ducks. A flock of pelicans snapped their long bills and chased carp, flapping their wings as they gulped the fish down.

My breathing slowed. Water always calmed me. It didn't matter too much what kind of water — ocean, lakes, rivers, swimming pool. I just love it. I wanted to dive in and wash away everything that had just happened. But I remembered what Dad had said about treated effluent, or poo, being pumped into Lake Warrong. Much as I would have loved a swim, I didn't fancy swimming in that.

I rolled my rusty BMX down the hill, dodging bottlebrushes and gum trees, leant my bike against the huge cement drain, and headed for the water's edge.

Weaving through the bullrushes, with an eye out for snakes, I thrust my hand into my pocket — my tennis ball. I must have shoved it in there before I left the house. I pulled it out and tossed it in the air. Some catching practice would be good for me and would take my mind off Mum and Seal Point. Anyway, if I couldn't go to Seal Point, I'd just have to work on my ball skills. That was Plan B.

Plan A was to show Matt and Josh that our family was cool enough to stay at Seal Point. Once they saw how well I swam, surfed and snorkeled, I hoped they'd accept me as a friend and stop calling me 'Fatguts' and 'Oops'.

Plan B was to improve my catching and batting and kicking and marking. At first Plan A seemed like the easy option, especially as I pretty much hate ball sports, but after the latest puffer fish attack, Plan B was looking better all the time.

You see, Wilton is sport-mad — actually ball-sport-mad. Golf, cricket, bowls, tennis, footy — so long as you're good at sport, you're in. Everyone loves you. That's OK for Justin, Mr All-round-sportsman, cricket captain and best-and-fairest in his footy league, but it's tough for me. Tough because Justin is two years younger than me and tough because I don't like footy or cricket. People running around screaming and hurting each other, and chucking hard leather balls is not my idea of fun. It's the same old thing every week.

'Do it for the team!'

'Go in hard!'

'Kick it long!'

'Dropped catches lose matches!'

Don't they ever get sick of it?

The instructions are always a little different when I play.

'Keep those drinks cold, kid.'

'Run these oranges out to the huddle, mate.'

Drinks or oranges. According to everyone in Wilton, the 'other kid from the shop' can't kick and can't catch . I have no sport sense, 'no eye for it', or something. If I was honest, I'd say they're right.

I'm a good swimmer though. Freestyle is my favourite stroke and I'm a pretty good backstroker. If only this town had a heated pool, any pool, they'd see the 'other kid from the shop' was good at something too. I'd dive in and slice through the water like Ian Thorpe, water foaming behind me — only I'm not very fast and Ian Thorpe doesn't have floppy guts.

I go to Little Athletics and love throwing the discus, but I hate all the other stuff like sprints, hurdles and long jumps. The coaches are bossy and grumpy.

Maybe if I was tall and skinny like Justin I'd like sport more and be better at it. Mum says my problem is I don't try hard enough and I'm 'podgy'. She watches with hard eyes as I eat and nags me when she decides I've had enough. Dad tells her to leave me alone. From my bedroom I hear him hissing. Sometimes I can make out what he's saying, '… like me. He's fine … it's just puppy fat.'

Dad tries to help me with sport too, but he doesn't have much time now we have the shop.

When I'm not stacking or cleaning shelves, I toss the tennis ball against the back wall and try to catch it.

'Good for getting your eye in, mate,' says Dad. Good for twisting your ankle and crashing into the back fence, I reckon.

Still, if I can get my eye in, whatever that means, I might be better at sport and then Plan B would work. Matt and Josh would let me be their friend.

Tim Franklin reckons I'm mad to want to be friends with Matt and Josh. He reckons they're bullies and dumb. But Matt and Josh are the most popular kids in our class and I want to be popular too.

I started patting the ball in the air with my right hand, then my left. So far so good. I tried tossing the ball in the air and catching it one-handed. Pretty good. Maybe my eye was finally going in! Time for the tough ones — lobs!

I tossed the ball high into the sky and positioned myself for the catch. I looked up, keeping my eye on the ball like Dad says, when the sun burst from behind a cloud. I couldn't see a thing. I staggered around, blinded, until my eyes cleared. I saw my fluffy old ball land with a plop and roll into the cement culvert. Plan B wasn't looking so good.

'Great! Can anything else go wrong today?' I muttered as I lurched after my ball. In the mud and sludge at the mouth of the drain my feet took on a life of their own and flew out from under me. I landed on my bum with a wet splat. Thick ooze coated my legs and Nikes.

'Gross! Stinks more than Dad's socks!' I yelled, covering my mouth and nose with my hand. I grabbed the gum-tree branch that hung over the muck and hoisted myself to my feet. I wasn't a pretty sight. Every time I thought I had my footing, I slipped, skated and slid back into the mud. I felt like one of the Three Stooges, those guys in the slapstick videos Dad makes us watch.

On my third downward slide, I grabbed the drain wall, steadied myself and pulled until I could step inside the drain. At my feet were a half-eaten pigeon, torn chip packets, bleached and crumpled

Coke cans, and matted weeds. I screwed up my face. Disgusting!

Deeper in the drain the tennis ball lay next to a mouldy hamburger, limp lettuce spilling out from between the bun halves.

'Stuff the ball.' It wasn't worth the effort, or the smell. I gripped the drain roof and picked my way over the garbage back into the sunshine. That's when my mum's voice started. 'Money doesn't grow on trees, Cam. How do you think we are going to replace that?' Mum's shark voice thrashed around in my head. It happens all the time. I can hear her telling me whenever I do anything wrong. Who needs a conscience?

'Shut up!' I yelled. My voice echoed along the dark drain. I sighed. There was no question about it, I'd have to get my ball.

Keeping one hand on the drain wall, I tiptoed back, placing my feet between matted gunk and slimy sludge. My feet skidded and slipped until I was level with my ball. I poked the hamburger aside with the toe of my Nike, pinched my nose and reached for the ball.

It's hard to balance when you're holding your nose and leaning forward. I fell flat on my face. Stinking, cold mud covered my face and filled one of my ears. The mouldy hamburger squished against the corner of my mouth. I pulled myself to my feet, shook the putrid gunk from my ball and wiped my face with my forearm. I spat the black seaweed taste from my mouth and flipped the ball in my hand.

'All that for a ball!' My once pale-green T-shirt had turned cow-poo green, my shorts, heavily caked with mud, hung to my knees and thick mud was gathering in muddy lumps on my socks and shoes. 'She'll go nuts!'

I wobbled to my feet and froze. Ahead in the drain, soft light glowed like a street lamp on a foggy night.

Drains don't have lights in them. The longer the drain, the blacker it became — at least, that's the way it was supposed to be. A weird light in a stinky drain was far more exciting than heading home to go another round with a furious puffer fish. Excitement bubbled in my chest.

'Nothing ventured,' I muttered. I wasn't sure what it meant. Dad said it lately when he had to ask Mum a question: 'Nothing ventured, nothing gained'.

I couldn't get any dirtier, so I strode forward through the grunge. The mud slurping under my feet sounded like Justin finishing a thickshake.

Ahead the light grew larger, glowing soft and golden instead of harsh and white like summer sunshine. It was like I'd been tied to a rope and someone was hauling me in.

A twig snapped, bringing my gaze from the light to the drain floor. Instead of mud and sludge, twigs, dry grass and leaves littered the cement drain. I prodded the floor with my foot to check it was solid and safe. All clear. Another couple of steps forward and the air changed. I sniffed deeply, tasting it. The stink of decay and mould had disappeared, replaced by the smell of sunshine and dry grass.

I had to keep going. Four quick steps and the cement disappeared. Packed dirt, tree roots and boulders bulged out from the walls and ceilings.

My feet padded and scraped as the leaves, grasses and straw gave way to a hard dirt floor. I squatted like one of those TV explorers and took a closer look. The drain had become a tunnel.

I looked back over my shoulder to check I could still see the drain and daylight. The mouth of the drain, shining white, was now only the size of a basketball. Ten more steps and the tunnel narrowed, becoming so small I had to crawl to keep going. A short shuffle and it opened to a huge cave.

'Cool.'

I'd read about secret caves in books, but I'd never thought I'd find one! It had to be a secret cave; everyone in Wilton knew everything about the place, plus people told you everything they knew, even if you didn't want to hear. It had to be a secret cave or someone would have told me about it by now.

I laughed. Cam, the crappy cricketer and dud footballer, had found something special. Excitement flooded my stomach. My knees wobbled so hard I had to hold them. Perhaps my cave could be Plan C …

The cave was about the size of two tennis courts and filled with golden light. Its earth walls were dotted with rocks of all sizes; tree roots, knotted and messy like morning hair, hung from the ceiling.

And the floor ...

I gasped and leant back against the cool wall. The floor was completely covered in polished glass, twisted metal, fishing hooks and shiny plastic of every colour imaginable. It reminded me of the bower-bird nest I'd seen on Grandpa's farm in Gippsland, except that the bower bird's stuff was all blue. This was red, blue, mauve, gold, cream, green — I couldn't even guess the names of some of the colours.

I looked up. The gold light that filled the cave shone down through a round hole in the cave roof. It looked like a window, but was covered with a yellowish fabric instead of glass. The edges were puckered and held in place by twisted tree roots.

My eyes followed the light from the ceiling to a pile of dry leaves and branches below. The heap was as large as one tennis court, but round and made up of willow branches, bullrushes, gum leaves and seed pods, all twisted together like a basket — woven, I think you call it. Gumnuts, spiky seed pods and pine cones were crammed into gaps, stuck there with mud that looked like chocolate mousse. Straw, the same stuff that covered the tunnel floor, stuck out like tufts of hair between the sticks.

I had to go closer — get a better look. I checked out the cave for a moment, looking for a clear path to the pile of branches. Nothing. I had to cross the coloured sea.

It was noisy going. Pops, squeaks and crunches filled the air. Whoever or whatever lived in this cave would know I was here now!

The pile of branches and twigs turned out to be a knee-high wall that surrounded five more circles — each a different colour and each sloping down towards the centre. It reminded me of something — a nest! It looked like a giant nest and in the middle of it lay a glittering egg-shaped thing, about the size of Dad's small filing cabinet. I glanced around the cave again to make sure I was still alone, and stepped over the nest wall.

Boy, someone had been busy. Bike handlebars and chains, flattened drink cans, screws, bolts and tool handles, all polished and shining, filled the second and silver circle of the nest. I tiptoed across it to the next layer, cringing as screeches and crunches echoed around the cave.

This circle was completely filled with pink stuff. Glass, bits of rope, feathers, plastic and scraps of fabric lay scattered in a wide ring, each overlapping the next. I rubbed my neck. All that looking over my shoulder was starting to hurt.

The pink layer didn't make much noise as I tiptoed across it to the next layer where everything was a different shade of yellow — some like a new duckling, others as pale as the cheese Mum and Dad eat. Blankets, bits of lambskin like the one I slept on when I was a baby, balls of wool and scraps of jumpers flattened under my feet as I moved towards the egg-thing and the final circle.

The closer I went, the more the centre circle glittered and shone. Jewels! It was completely filled with jewels. Sapphires, diamonds, green stones and red ones, like the one in Mum's engagement ring, lay among pearls, bits of gold and opals. Some stones were as big as my hand, others so small four would have just covered my fingernail. Gold chains as thick as my wrist, and others as fine as babies' hair, slithered among the gems like silent, glowing snakes. Gold and silver rings, some set with stones and others as plain as Dad's wedding band, poked out from between the jewels. Modern jewellery, like the stuff Mum stares at in catalogues, and old necklaces and rings, like those you see in King Arthur movies, lay together. There had to be thousands — no, millions of dollars' worth of jewellery lying at my feet.

My brain raced with ideas. I could fill my pockets and sell the jewels — use the money to buy our old house and move back to Beldare. Better still, we could buy a huge new house or build a dream house in Beldare. Well, my dream home — after all, I'd found the treasure. I could go to school at St Anne's again and catch the bus home with Jacob, Sam and Nick, like I used to. Mum could go back to work for Dobsons' law firm and I could go to Nick's house until Mum finished work every Monday, Tuesday and Friday.

Dad could get a job at a different bank. Just because Regional Bank Victoria had made him redundant didn't mean other banks wouldn't want him. I'd heard Mum telling her friends at tennis that several banks were interested in him. 'He's an excellent manager … 'Course he'd never tell you that. Too modest,' she'd said to Mrs Jackson. And if he had to own a store, he could buy one in the city, a big one, like a supermarket or something, and employ lots of staff.

The pool! I could join the squad again! And get a new puppy. The possibilities were endless. We'd all be back in Beldare. Mum would be happy and the puffer fish could swim out to sea, never to be seen again.

I planned, schemed and even mapped out my dream home — well, I started to. The egg-shaped thing kept distracting me. It sat up like an American grid-iron football waiting to be kicked. It wasn't its size which distracted me but the five separate colours. Each circled the egg, brighter and more alive than any rainbow. The bottom ring glistened like a glossy horse in the sunlight, the next shimmered like fish scales, the third was a bright red-pink and the second last circle gleamed as golden as the chains twinkling at my feet. The final layer was a combination of all the colours, but more brilliant. It shone and shimmered like glitter on a Christmas card.

I squatted and stared at the egg-thing. The nest! The egg had the same colours, in the same order, as the nest. What creature would create a nest like this and lay such an incredible egg?

The egg drew me closer. I had to touch it. I needed to know if it was warm like skin or cold like stone. Jewels squeaked under my feet. I heard a flap or flutter. I paused. In the silence of the cave the thudding of my heart filled my ears. I looked around me. Nothing had changed. I was still alone.

I turned back to the egg. Its outer shell appeared to be thick and looked as smooth as polished wood. I reached out to feel it.

'GET BACK SSSSS, YOU EVIL MAN-BOY, SSSSSSS!'

The voice filled the huge cave, bouncing off the rocks, crashing from the glittering floor to the ceiling. It spun around and around me like a fierce wind, knocking me to the nest-floor. The air had become thick like cotton wool. I could smell smoke — the kind from a crackling, open fire — and I could feel flames licking at my face and legs. I peered around the cave, looking for a fire or the voice's owner. Nothing but the shiny floor, rocky walls and a huge boulder at the back. Icy fear filled my stomach.

'Sssss how did you find my drag-egg, ssss?'

I dropped my head between my knees and pressed the heel of my hands into my ears. I'd heard people could get ear bleeds from really loud noise. My throat hurt and I couldn't swallow. What on earth could make a noise so powerful?

Time to be brave.

'I only —' Great, I was whimpering like a terrified dog.

'SSSSSilencccce!' I rolled forward, my forehead pressing into the jewels. Rubies and stuff are really sharp! They hurt more than Justin's elbows.

'Sssstannnd up, man-boy.'

The volume dropped a little, but the voice still sounded like its owner wanted to rip my head off. I leapt to my feet and brushed the jewels from my shoes, shorts and forehead. I tried to look like I was doing it as fast as I could.

While I dusted myself down, I stole looks around the cave out of the corner of my eye. The nest, the floor, the entrance to the cave were all the same. Except ... the huge boulder against the cave's back wall was gone.

'Don't bother looking for me, man-boy ssssss.'

I shut my eyes and listened hard, like I do when I play murder-in-the-dark with Justin and his friends. If you close your eyes you can sometimes work out where a sound is coming from.

'How did you ssss find my home ssss?'

I cleared my throat to answer, but the voice boomed over me.

'No matter sssss. You have found me, sssso

now I will have to decide what I will do with you sss.'

The cold, sharp fear that gripped my stomach flowed into my legs. Do with me? What did that mean? This was too much. I had only come here to find my tennis ball. Finding the cave was a fluke. I didn't mean any harm. Maybe if I explained, the noise would understand and let me go.

'I was only looking. I've never seen anything so beautiful. I just…'

'Enough, man-boy. Sssstep out of my nesssst.'

I wobbled and stumbled over the jewels, the blankets and lambskins, the pink glass and plastic and the polished metal, and climbed over the woven wall. As I did, a jewel, as red as fire and as large as my hand, fell out of the cuff on my shorts and clattered to the cave floor. I bent down and scooped it up, holding it out on my open palm towards the voice.

'I missed one. I'll just take it back.'

'NO!'

The air rattled and hissed. I heard something scrape in the back of the cave and could feel movement over my head. A squealing wind buffeted me; a wind that stank of roast beef, rotting flesh and something else — something icy-cold like the smell of the ice-cream freezer at The Corner Store. Blackness swooped from the cave roof.

I yelped. My palm felt like it had been burnt by a hot poker. I held it to my chest, too scared to look and see what had happened to it.

'Now, ssssssshall I eat you?'

I really wanted to be brave, to face death bravely like heroes do in books, but I didn't want to die. I had to tell Mum I was sorry, that I really didn't hate her or Justin. I had to apologise to Justin for calling him a 'Mummy's boy' this morning. I opened my mouth and shut it again like a carp thrown on a river bank. No words would come out. I stared at the brightly coloured cave floor, tears melting the pinks and blues into purple. I tried to think of something to say — anything, but still I made like a fish. I could only think of flashing claws, torn flesh and dripping blood.

I was on death's doorstep, about to knock, and I couldn't find a single word to save myself.

'I'm sorry. It's so beautiful here. I didn't mean any harm.' I whispered to the floor, wondering what my mum would say when they found my bones — if they ever did.

Rattling, hissing and scraping wrapped around me like a cold wind. Goose bumps prickled my arms. What was it? A monster? A deranged mental patient? Or just some of the tough kids from Wilton West? Maybe it was a bunyip?

The rattling closed in and the air grew colder. The smell of roast beef, rotting flesh and ice returned.

Hell! If I was going to die, I would at least look up and see my killer. The image of the West kids returned. I hoped it wasn't them playing some trick. I'd never, ever make friends if this got out! The gluggy smell settled upon my shoulders, making me want to throw up.

I lifted my eyes. A huge blurry image came sharply into focus.

Brown eyes, the colour of chocolate and as

large as basketballs stared at me; long lashes as thick as my little finger fluttered with each blink; nostrils flared and snorted, white teeth gleamed, and foamy saliva dripped to the floor. Black pointy claws, like a giant eagle's talons, gripped pieces of pink and blue plastic. Light bounced and shimmered off the creature's silver body, throwing thousands of tiny rainbows around the cave.

'A dragon!' I whispered. The words felt heavy and baggy — too big for me. Dragons didn't exist. They were make-believe creatures, not real. I shook my head and shut my eyes. When I opened them, the dragon still stared at me. Its eyes softened. I thought I saw a flicker of fear cross them.

Instead of thoughts of sorrow and death, a thousand questions bubbled in my brain.

'Clossse your mouth, man-boy sss. Haven't you sssseen a dragon before sss?'

'N-n-no.'

'Well, now you have sssss. Damnation!' The dragon glared at me and began muttering. 'This was not a wise idea. What am I to do with him ssss?' It thrust its face into mine, snapped its head back and opened its mouth. My last sight alive was to be flashing white teeth, smelly yellow saliva and blood-red gums.

'Wait! I won't tell anyone about you or the egg, I promise.'

'Drag-egg!' The dragon squinted at me. 'Man-boy, sss your kind doesss not know the meaning of the word "promisssse".'

'I do. Please, I won't tell … m-m-maybe I can help you.' I looked around the cave, desperate to find something I could do to save my life.

'What help could you possibly be? I am a dragon ssss. I need no help from a puny man-boy ssss. Though you do look a tasty morsel. Damnation … why did I take that oath?'

'I could clean your cave …' I clawed my brain for jobs. I help Mum with the cooking and the dishes; maybe a dragon needs that sort of help. 'I could bring you food. I could guard your egg. Please, please.' I reached out to the dragon like Mr Androtious, the Greek greengrocer at the local market — only the greengrocer pleaded with us to buy his fruit; I was pleading for my life.

'Do not beg! Your kind love to beg!' roared the dragon, smoke puffing from its mouth and spraying in my face. It stepped back and looked at me. For the first time I could see all of its chest and front legs. It was covered in scales the size of Dad's palm. Each shimmered and twinkled like the top multicoloured layer of the egg. 'There may be something you can do for me.'

I sighed a huge sigh of relief and smiled a watery smile.

'I wasss wrong,' hissed the dragon. 'You can be of no help to me ssss. Leave ssss. Leave before I change my mind ssss.'

I turned and crawled out of the tunnel, slipping and sliding, skidding and sloshing, terrified the dragon was playing with me like a cat with a mouse. I jumped on my bike and pedalled like crazy. My head thumped and my heart was an old steam train clattering in my chest. My legs felt like someone else's while my mind darted from one terrified thought to the next.

Saved from the foaming, slimy, glistening teeth. But why?

three

'Cameron, you're filthy!' raged the puffer fish. Purple veins snaked across her forehead, her eyelids fluttered and her fingers twitched. Her face was as red as a weight-lifter going for gold. 'What on earth have you been doing?'

I stared at my mud-encrusted shoes. It was my turn to act like a fish — a fish out of water. I stood there opening and shutting my mouth. I shrugged. Not a good move. Mum cut loose, bigtime. She roared about my clothes, my attitude, the way I looked at her and even the way I stood. I knew she had more to come too. She hadn't even started on the pre-dragon fight.

'I can't remember being so disappointed in you. First this morning's episode and now this.' A fine spray of her saliva settled on my face. I resisted the urge to wipe it off. 'Well, Cam? How did you get so dirty?'

I thought about telling her that I was nearly dragon lunch, but the truth was so hard to believe I wasn't sure I believed it myself. There was no choice, I had to lie. Before I started, Dad burst through the door that separated the shop from our house.

'For God's sake, Barb, keep your voice down,' he hissed through tight, twisted lips. 'You're scaring the customers.'

Mum turned to face him, hands clutching her hips and eyes flashing. She hissed back, 'Look at him, John.'

'Ease up, love, all boys get dirty. I'll deal with it later.' Dad slammed the door and was gone. Mum made weird 'oh' and 'well' noises before continuing her attack on me, only this time so quietly I missed half of what she said. I wasn't brave enough to say 'Pardon?'. I just nodded and stared at the floor.

'Cameron! I asked how you got so filthy!'

Lie time. The only problem was I hadn't had time to plan my story. I'd been so relieved to have survived that I hadn't considered what I'd tell Mum. This had to be good. I took a deep breath and launched into it.

'It was horrible, Mum. I rode down to the lake and was hanging out near that big drain thing when this bunch of West boys jumped me.' Mum knew all about the West boys. The old ladies buying magazines and jelly babies knew about the tough West boys. In fact, everyone in Wilton knew about the West boys. I'd never met one, but I knew they were big trouble. 'They pulled me off my bike and chucked me in the drain.' To force my point I worked in a chin quiver and a voice wobble. It wasn't hard considering I'd just faced death at the fangs of a mythical creature.

Mum's face crumpled and her hands dropped from her hips.

'They held me under the water and I thought I'd drown.' I ran my fingers through my dry hair and realised my lie was fast becoming unbelievable.

'Cam, they could have killed you!' She rushed forward and began prodding my hair, squeezing my arms and staring into my eyes. 'Are you sure you're okay? No cuts? Nothing sore? Did you swallow much mud?' She forced my mouth open and peered down my throat.

'No, Mum. I'm okay, just a bit shook-up.' That wasn't a lie!

Mum put her hand on my shoulder. 'Do you know any of them, Cam? They can't get away with this sort of thing.' She used the thick voice that made her eyebrows all crinkly — at least, I think she did. I stared at my shoes, just in case 'liar' was printed all over my face in big, fat, black texta. If Mum found out I was lying … well, I'd rather face the dragon.

'Please don't do anything, Mum. It'll only make it worse.' The quake in my voice was for real this time.

She sighed, fidgeted with her wedding ring and then dropped the 'hot pursuit'.

'Cam, I know you've just had an awful fright, but we need to talk about what happened earlier. You threw an order book at me and said some terrible things. I can't and won't put up with that. I would like an apology and, of course, there has to be punishment.' Mum stepped back, fidgeting with her wedding ring.

I nodded and waited. Her punishments were usually pretty tough. She took a deep breath. 'You're to hang out the washing and bring it in, do the dishes and vacuum the house for the next two weeks.' She sighed a long deep sigh and rubbed her forehead with her thumb and first finger. 'And Cam, no television for the rest of the week.' She paused and I steadied myself for the list to continue. Instead she sighed again and said, 'Go clean yourself up and stay in your room for a bit. I want you to think about what you said.'

I rushed down the hall to the bathroom before she changed her mind and added to the list. My punishments weren't too bad really. I wonder if parents ever punish themselves? At school, if two kids throw things at each other, both children get into trouble. Mum did start the throwing with that red pen. Still, I wasn't about to point that out and risk further punishment.

I hope she never finds out I lied. I think I heard her hiss-whisper something about inquiries and West boys as I rushed off to the bathroom. I hoped she didn't inquire too well. I don't know who I'd back if the dragon came across Mum doing the puffer-fish thing.

• • •

It took me ages in the shower to wash all that stinky gunk off. I found mud in places where I didn't know I had places.

Wrapped in a towel, I crept into my bedroom and shut the door with a soft click. I leaned against the door, staring out the window and thinking about my old bedroom in Beldare. It had been really big and open with windows that reached from the ceiling to the polished wood floor.

My room had been 'summer ocean blue' and 'sunburst lemon yellow'. Mum had taken me shopping after school to choose the paint, curtains and matching doona cover. I have to admit it looked pretty good, like one of those rooms in the magazines Mum loves. The walls were a bit plain until Mum bought some framed *Star Wars* posters without my having to ask. The wood in the frame was the same colour as my bed and the floor.

When we lived there I thought my room was pretty ordinary, but now — looking around my new room — I knew it had been great. Best of all, it had been *my* room and I didn't have to share it with Justin.

I sighed. The image of my old room faded and once again I was staring at the once white, but now sand-coloured, venetians, lilac walls and pink floral carpet. I still had my *Star Wars* posters and my Ian Thorpe poster. Dad had put them up the day we moved in. They cheered the place up a bit, but Justin's Collingwood doona and posters kind of swamped the room and made it dark and gloomy. All that black can make you feel pretty low.

Mum and Dad had put up a little shelf for my *Star Wars* models and my framed swimming certificates. I had a couple of books on the shelf, my favourites like *Misery Guts* and *Rowan of Rin*, but the rest of my books were still packed in huge boxes in the spare room. We didn't have enough room for most of our stuff in this house.

Justin needed three shelves to hold his autographed footy and cricket bat, footy and cricket trophies and the ball he bowled a hat trick with. It was like living in a sports museum.

One look and you could tell two people shared the room. Not a thing was out of place in Justin's half. His bed and cupboard looked like another photo from one of Mum's magazines. Mine looked like the 'before' shot — socks, jocks, T-shirts, a trackie and — even though school had finished two weeks ago — my school shoes peeking out from under the bed like naughty kids.

And if you still hadn't worked out two kids slept here, the toilet paper divider was a dead giveaway.

Justin hated my mess. Two months ago

Mum and Dad had gone off about 'the state of our room' and sent us to tidy it up. That led to words, socks and punches being thrown. Justin stormed off to the bathroom and came back with a toilet roll. He drew a line down the middle of the room with chalk, then stuck the toilet paper to the floor with thumb tacks. I must stay on my side and he must stay on his. I'm allowed in his half to come in the door but, apart from that, his half is a no-go zone, punishable by dead arm or leg or both, depending on how badly the rule is broken. 'Course, if Justin could see me now, leaning against the door, which is in his half of the room, I'd qualify for both.

Only the built-in robes and computer weren't divided because we both use them. The computer was Dad's, but the government introduced a new tax system just after we moved so Dad had to update the computer as well as buy new software. His new computer is crammed in a corner in the lounge room, just behind Mum's wing-back chair. Justin and I scored the old one. It's squeezed between our beds, on top of an old door balanced between our bedside tables. It looks weird but makes a pretty good desk. Dad even arranged for a new phone line to be hooked up so we could use the Internet in our room. I think it was a kind of peace offering after the big move.

Being banished to my room wasn't such a bad thing because it gave me a chance to search the Internet for information about dragons.

Wow, there are some dragon freaks around! I found pages and pages of stuff about fire-breathing dragons; water dragons; lizard dragons and people-eating dragons; dragons that guard gold; dragons that spit acid, and multicoloured dragons; European dragons; Occidental dragons; Oriental dragons; British dragons and Mediterranean dragons; dragon anatomy; dragon diets and dragon young. I read about knights, gold and princesses; the Bible, battles and sacrifices.

Though the sites disagreed on many things, they all agreed dragons were cunning, bad-tempered, territorial, vengeful, greedy and terrifying.

I learnt heaps but I still couldn't find the answers to my main questions. I needed to know if dragons lived in Australia and, most of all, I wanted proof that dragons really existed. Apart from being more wary, I still didn't have any answers.

Maybe I'd dreamt it. Maybe the whole thing had been a trick of my imagination. Maybe I had a fever — was getting sick or something. Or maybe I'd been so angry with Mum that I'd made the whole thing up. I shut down the computer, flopped on my bed and stared at the ceiling.

I relived every minute of the morning, from the moment I first lost my ball down the drain, to my incredible escape. The smells — smoke, roast beef, ice, rotting meat and dry warm air. The sounds — the rattle, hiss, crunch under my feet, and the voice — I *knew* I heard the voice because my ears were still ringing. The things I touched — the prickle of the edge of the nest, the cool, smooth ruby and the pain of my burnt palm.

I lifted my hand to examine it. The skin was puckered and blistered. Watery stuff oozed from beneath white, torn skin. I touched it. 'Ouch!' I squealed as pain shot down from my fingertips to my shoulder.

I had to go back. I had to see if the dragon, its nest and huge egg thing were real, and I wanted to do it first thing tomorrow.

This time I'd be better prepared.

I just hoped it wasn't an acid-spitting, vengeful, people-eating dragon.

four

Mum and Justin had gone shopping for stuff for Justin to take to Seal Point, and Dad was phoning distributors from the shop phone. I crept out of the house.

I didn't bother with my jobs before I left. Washing clothes in the face of death seemed stupid. I grabbed my backpack — filled with a tattered T-shirt, shorts and my old runners, a torch, some string and my pocket knife — and hitched the pack over my shoulder. I'm not sure why I'd packed a torch and string, but I figured they'd be useful for something.

The ride to the lake was tough going. Every time I put my burnt hand on the handlebars I yelped with pain, so I had to steer with one hand. After a wobbly ride, I hid my bike under the same bush beside the drain. I changed into old gear, shoved the torch, string and pocketknife into my pocket, and wedged the backpack under the front wheel of my bike.

It took less time to scramble through the drain to the tunnel than it had yesterday, probably because I wasn't worried about getting dirty — the creature in the cave bothered me more than Mum's growling.

Before I knew it, I'd stepped out of the sludge onto the dry path to the dragon's cave. My knees wobbled and my heart thudded in my ears like bongo drums. I wiped my sweaty palms on my shorts and immediately regretted it. Pain throbbed in my burnt palm and spread into my fingers.

'No turning back now,' I muttered, hoping it might make me feel even braver.

I dropped to my knees and crawled forward. A piece of blue metal jabbed my burnt hand and I knew I'd entered the cave.

I stood, cradling my hand against my chest, and gazed around. All looked the same as it had yesterday — floor littered with brightly coloured bits and pieces, a shallow nest of five circles and an egg, or drag-egg, shining in the middle. The air felt dry and warm. I breathed deeply — no roast beef, ice, rotting meat or smoke.

'D-D-D-Dragon, it's me, Cameron. We met yesterday.' My voice echoed around the cave, clattered against the roof and charged back at me.

Good one, idiot. We met yesterday? More like you nearly scared me stupid and threatened to eat me yesterday.

A rattle? My eyes darted around the cave. Nothing, except the huge boulder. It'd been there yesterday when I entered the cave, then it had disappeared. Today the boulder was back against the wall. I stepped towards it. I wanted to touch it, feel it — make sure it was a boulder and not — what? What else could it be?

I grimaced as each step filled the silent cave with pops, crunches and squeaks. As I neared the boulder, I reached out and poked it with my fingers, then traced a line across it. It felt warm and lumpy, like goose bumps.

Under my finger tips the boulder began to twist and turn, changing shape like a sock giving way to a foot, but, unlike the sock, the boulder changed colour from stone grey to pink to blue as it bulged and shuddered. With a hiss and a rattle, the boulder became the dragon.

I squealed like a little kid and sprinted for the tunnel.

'Did I frighten you, man-boy?'

I froze. The dragon rattled its bulk towards me. It made a weird noise in its throat, kind of like a cough. Its eyes twinkled. A deep rumbling started and rolled around the cave like thunder. I dropped to my knees. Here we go again. Time to die. Death must be very loud. I wrapped my arms around my head. The thunder crashed from ceiling to floor. Little gaps started between the crashes — gaps filled with snorts and gasps. I raised my head, just a tiny bit; the dragon was leaning against the cave wall. Its eyes were closed and blue tears splashed down its nose. Foaming drool spilled from its mouth.

'So what brings you back here, man-boy?' Wisps of smoke escaped from the dragon's mouth as it gasped for breath.

'I'm not sure.' I didn't know where to look. What if it was bad manners to look directly at a dragon? Or what if it was bad manners to keep your eyes turned down in the presence of a dragon? And what if it thought I was staring at the slobber dripping from its mouth? What if I caused my own death by a misplaced glance?

'Stop fidgeting!' It settled to the floor, resting its head on its front paws, or claws or whatever you call dragon feet. 'Do you always fidget so much?' It wiped a blue tear from its scaly snout.

'Yes, well — no. I just…'

It made that sound again — the cough, chuckle sort of thing in the back of its throat. Its body heaved and rattled with each chug.

'You are an odd one. I gave you your life yesterday and yet you return. Why, man-boy?'

'I thought I might have imagined you.'

Again with the throat noises! Surely it wasn't laughing at me?

'No one imagines us correctly, yet here you are, man-boy, looking at a real dragon and you don't believe.' It snorted and stretched its neck forward. Its chocolate eyes stared at me. 'Tell me about yourself.'

'My name is Cameron Mason. We — my mum, dad, brother Justin and I — moved here about six months ago —'

'How do you like living in a shop?'

'It's OK. Dad's always busy ...' My words hung in the air. I hadn't mentioned the shop.

'When he worked for the bank and you lived in Beldare he worked long hours too, did he not?'

Again I made like a gasping carp. How could it know about Dad's hours? Could be a lucky guess, but Beldare? Too freaky.

'Don't look so stunned. We dragons have special ways, man-boy.'

'I know. Your spit is acid,' I blurted. Good one. I hung my head, waiting for an attack, but it only chugged in its throat again, its body heaving. Definitely laughter. This overgrown lizard was laughing at me!

'You are a funny one, Cameronduncanmason.' My full name! I knew I'd only said Cameron Mason, not including the Duncan. What was going on? The dragon pawed the ground and held its sides. 'I look forward to telling the DDC about this.' It chortled and chuckled some more, then sighed and wiped its eyes, like Dad when he watches that comedian, Billy Connolly. 'Ah dear. Thank you, Cameronduncanmason. I cannot remember the last time I laughed so much.'

Great! I wasn't going to be eaten; instead I'd spend the rest of my life in a cage as a jester to amuse a dragon, a fire-breathing dragon with a weird sense of humour. This was getting out of hand. I'd risked my life and my mother's foul temper, come very close to peeing my pants, and all I got for my trouble was laughter. I could go to school and throw a cricket ball and get the same response. I didn't need it from a moody fantasy creature with disgusting breath.

'Look, Dragon —'

'Before you continue, Cameronduncanmason, stop wasting your time on the Internet. If you have a question, ask me.'

My anger dried up like a summer-rain puddle. How on earth did it know this stuff? I wanted to yell at it, ask it what was going on, but I didn't want to go back on the menu just when it seemed I'd come off. Instead of asking about the mind reading, I went for the safe question. 'Okay, why don't you tell me something about you?'

'My name is Dracofir. I am a European dragon, descendant of Fmau the Fantastic and Dracodwar of the Danes. I'm a dragoness, not an *it*, and I am 234 years old. I breathe fire, fly and, yes, I eat people — at least I used to. The DDC put a stop to that!' Her scaly brow furrowed. 'Harm our reputation, they said. Not in the spirit of peace and reconciliation, or some such rot. Hmph.' The twinkle bled from her eyes and she lowered her head to her feet. Silence filled the cave.

The DDC? Deadly Dragon Company? Dangerous Deadly Creatures? Death, Destruction,

Carnage? Don't Die, Cameron? I wasn't about to ask.

She jerked her head up and her eyes began to shine once more. 'And, Cameronduncanmason, my spit is no more acid than yours, though your breath is far worse than mine. What do you eat?'

My breath! I'd only just cleaned my teeth. Surely my breath was minty fresh. I puffed into my palm and sniffed. Yep! Smelt like mint. Her breath made me want to throw up! Smoke, roast beef, rotting meat and ice. I opened my mouth to tell her that her breath stank, but she cut me off.

'Now, do you still think you can help me?'

'Dragafear —' I tried the word on for size. She cut me off with a half-snort, half-laugh.

'DRACK—OH—FUR.' She said it slowly, as if I was a bit thick. She cocked her head and watched me try again.

'Dracofir.'

'Well done, man-boy. Continue.'

'Dracofir, I thought I could help you look after that.' I pointed to her nest and her drag-egg. 'Or gather some food or something.'

'But you have more than enough work awaiting you at home.'

This was starting to bug me! 'How do you know so much?'

'Things are not always simple, Cameronduncanmason. I told you, we dragons have special ways.'

'Have you been watching me?' Heat prickled my face.

'I suppose I have.' She raised her brow as she spoke.

'For how long?' I demanded, hands on my hips.

'Long enough to know your father lost his job at the bank, went to Seal Point for a weekend on his own to think about his future and returned to Beldare the proud owner of the Wilton Corner Store. I've watched you for long enough to know that you don't like Wilton and your mother is unhappy here too. I know she is giving you some … trouble and that you are fighting with your younger brother. I also know you haven't made friends and that you hoped a holiday in Seal Point would help.' She shifted her bulk and scratched at a shimmery scale with a black talon. 'I know you love swimming and miss the pool and you think you are a poor game player. Am I right?'

'Yes.' My head hung low and my hands dropped from my hips. This creature had just summed up my life in about five sentences. I felt as if I was standing naked in front of her.

'So do you think you can help me care for my drag-egg and keep up with all your other jobs, Cameronduncanmason?'

I looked straight into her warm eyes. 'I know I can.'

'Be back tomorrow morning before the bottom rays of the sun touch the tips of the pine tree, and tell no one where you are going.' Dracofir rose to her feet and turned to leave, dismissing me like Mrs Samson after she'd given me a neatness lecture. 'And, Cameronduncanmason, I'll know if you tell anyone, just as I know Justin is going to Seal Point. Your actions will show me your heart.' Dracofir turned back to her nest. 'I need to tend my drag-egg. Go now.'

five

Mum and Justin staggered out of bed, complaining about the noise, while I vacuumed the lounge room, put a load of washing in the machine, ate breakfast and did my dishes.

'Things to do,' I grinned as I dried the last dish.

'I'm impressed!' said Dad as he shot back into the shop.

'We'll see,' said Mum with a frown, tying the dressing gown cord around her waist.

I raced into my room before Mum could give me extra work, and finished packing my backpack. Butterflies flittered around inside my stomach. Maybe Dracofir and I could become friends and we could hang out together. I could visit her every day and learn more about dragons and stuff. Maybe she could teach me to read people's minds.

'I hope she likes it,' I muttered as I shook the bag and watched the package slip inside. I'd sneaked out to the twenty-four-hour supermarket last night, bought a gift for Dracofir — a peace offering I guess — and was back in bed by 9 pm. Justin and Mum had been too engrossed in some loud American TV show, *Friends* or *Sabrina* or something. I couldn't hear exactly what it was, only that fake laughter. Dad had been flat-out serving in the shop. Nobody knew I'd been and returned.

I slung the backpack onto my shoulder, grunting as I wiggled it into a comfortable spot. I peeked across the hall. Mum was twittering at a customer. Glass rattled in the drink refrigerator — Dad was restocking. Justin was going fishing with his friend Paul, so he'd be in the shed packing his gear. The coast was clear.

I stood in the kitchen and soaked up the sights of home, just in case the dragon decided to eat me after all. Lino, tiles and papers everywhere. Nothing like our kitchen in Beldare. It had been wood — Baltic pine, Mum called it — with a slate floor and clear benches. My tummy felt all twitchy.

I could hear Mum chirping goodbye to the customer. She sounded like a sparrow. The shop doorbell tinkled and for a moment there was silence — then Mum launched into a 'Dad-attack'. Something about working in the shop was demeaning, whatever that meant, and not as challenging as her old job. Great! I was about to go and face death, again, and the last thing I'd hear would be Mum nagging Dad.

I hitched my backpack and headed out of the house.

• • •

I'd figured the bottom of the sun would cross the pine trees by about nine o'clock. I squinted into the sky, then looked at my watch. Eight-thirty, and the sun still hadn't topped the trees. I was early. Being eaten for arriving late would be the final humiliation. I hid my bike, changed clothes behind spiky bottlebrush shrubs and stashed the backpack under the back wheel of my bike. With the package under my arm, I headed for the drain.

'D-D-D-Dracofir. It's me.' My voice echoed around the empty cave.

'You're early.' The cave had been empty, except for the nest and egg, and then Dracofir appeared, out of the air.

'I brought you a gift.' I unwrapped the package and laid it on the ground between us.

'Ham. You think humans taste like ham?' She shook her head and chuckled. 'How would you know?'

Embarrassment burned my face and anger seethed in my chest. That was it! I'd bought the leg of ham with my savings — every last bit of my savings. She could at least be a little grateful!

'You are very rude. Ham is … is … b-bloody dear. I spent all my money on that. Do you know how long it'll take me to save forty-three dollars again? And Mum would've killed me if she'd caught me sneaking —'

'Well, well, Cameronduncanmason, what a temper.'

'*Cam* will do — that's what my fr — family call me.' The 'f' word again. It stuck in my throat like too much peanut butter. 'I don't have a temper. I just think it's very rude not to be grateful when someone has gone out of their way to buy you a gift. I thought it would be hard for you to hunt your own food, with the egg-thing to look after and all. I read in a *Reader's Digest* once, when I was waiting for the dentist, that people taste like ham, and you said you used to eat people, so I —'

'Relax, man-boy. Damnation, but you are quick to anger. Yes, I do like the taste of humans, and I suppose they do taste a little hamish.' Dracofir rattled and hissed closer, bending her head to sniff at the ham. 'True, it is difficult for me to hunt while I care for my drag-egg. It is indeed fortunate we dragons only eat once every month or so. Ah, but when we do eat it is truly a feast — a feast of beef, or lamb or pork and many grasses and vegetables.' Her tongue rolled out of her mouth. 'Hmmm, thank you. I appreciate the thought.'

I smiled. I wondered if it looked as fake as it felt.

She stabbed the ham with a sharp claw and lumbered to the back of the cave. Her arrow-shaped tail swooshed past my nose. I think she was hiding her ham for later, kind of like a dog burying a bone.

'You kept your promise, Cameronduncanmason. You have returned before the bottom rays of the sun reached the tops of the pine tree and you told no one. Maybe you are different.' I think she smiled at me. All those glistening teeth, blood-red gums and colour-changing drool made it hard to be sure, but her eyes twinkled in a smiley sort of way. She moved back towards me and the mouth of the cave and settled her body on the glittering floor. She reminded me of a Labrador resting in its kennel.

'Dracofir, can I ask you a question?'

'But of course. I told you yesterday to ask rather than waste your time on the Internet. What do you need to know?'

'Yesterday you said something about the DDC. What is it?'

'Ahh, the Drakensberg Dragon Council. It is like your government, only better. Where your government is elected, our council members are automatically elevated to the DDC when they have proved themselves worthy. They uphold Dragon Lore and adapt existing laws to suit these troubled times. The DDC ensures we dragons are true to the council, the world, and to ourselves.'

'How do you become worthy?' I wasn't sure I really wanted to know, especially if it involved eating people.

'A worthy dragon is a dragon of virtue and strength — a dragon who has made a significant contribution to dragon society and has protected our environment. It may have rescued a weaker creature from destruction, or intervened to lessen the effects of a horrific event that threatened the earth.'

I grabbed the discarded wrapping from my gift and sat on it, protecting my bum from the sharp floor. 'I thought you dragons were more into burning and eating everything.'

'No, Cameronduncanmason, that is your role. It is our job to nurture new life and to protect the threatened, but our main responsibility is to care for the Springs of Life.' Her dark eyes held my gaze.

'Care for the what?'

'The Springs of Life. The very essence of all life on earth flows through these waters, both above and under the ground. They replenish the earth, create new life and growth. We dragons protect the source of the springs from risk and ensure they flow freely. If the Springs of Life should ever become blocked or dry ...'

'What would happen?' I blurted, frightened she wouldn't finish the story.

'The earth would die.' Dracofir's voice hung in the air. I fiddled with my shoelace. 'Do not worry, man-boy, we have been successful thus far.' Her lips pulled back from her teeth into what I figured was a smile.

I decided to get back onto the Drakensberg Dragon Council and off dying worlds.

'Dracofir, is the DDC a worldwide group?'

'Indeed. Over the past five hundred years dragon numbers dropped so far that dragon species had to join forces to create the Drakensberg Dragon Council for protection. People would do well to heed our unity.'

I understood what she meant. World peace was a big topic at school, but I didn't want to go down that road either, so I changed the subject again.

'So what are you doing in Australia, Dracofir?'

Not the right question. She jumped to her feet. The cave shook like a cardboard dolls' house. I was so used to the seesaw ride I didn't bother getting scared. I stood up, waited and watched.

'Sss I am here becaussse of you and your kind sss!' Her voice was low and even, kind of like Mum's shark voice. It made my ears burn. She thrust her snout in my face, panting like a dog after a long run. Dragon's breath was worse than disgusting! The roast meat smell returned, stronger than ever and with it came a dead smell, like the rotting cat Justin and I once found down by the lake. Dragons might have taken an oath not to eat people, but their breath was still a deadly weapon. I covered my mouth with my hand and tried not to spew on her dragon feet. Huge globs of spit pooled around my shoes. I hoped she was right about her spit not being acid.

Dracofir snorted and stepped back to glare at me. Her eyes were no longer chocolate brown, but as black as a crow, and just as spooky. I swallowed and waited. It would only take a stamp of her foot or a lash of her tail to kill me.

'Ssss you and your kind sssss are destroying our homesss. You threaten the Springsss of Life with your waysss.' The words flew at me. 'Ssss you are killing our earth ssss. There are sssso few placesss left for usss to dwell ssss.'

'But Dracofir, what have I done? I've never been outside Australia.' Fire, orange and hot, shot out of her nostrils. I leapt to my left. Flames blackened the cave wall behind me.

'You ssssstupid, sssstupid boy.' Her tail lashed

the ground, scattering coloured plastic and glass. 'How could I sssss think you could sssss help me?'

'I can help. I want to …' My voice was small.

'Ssss get out and don't come back ssss!' Dracofir stretched out her wings, flapped them twice and rose to the roof of the cave.

I hadn't seen her wings before. They were shaped like a bird's but had no feathers. Skin, as fine as tissue paper, stretched between the bones. I could see the veins and muscles work with each flap, while fine glittering dust fell to the cave floor. Dracofir perched on a ledge and folded her wings. She changed size again and was now much smaller — about as large as a Great Dane. Despite my fear I wondered how she could do that — change without my seeing it happen. I looked up at her. The look in her eyes filled me with sorrow.

'Go ssss,' she whispered.

I stumbled to my feet and sprinted from the cave into the tunnel, only stopping to change out of my muddy clothes before pedalling home.

six

'You were up and about early, mate.' Dad grinned across the shop counter, cleaning spray in one hand, cloth in the other. 'Mrs Johnston and Midge were in, asking after you.'

'Can I grab a drink, Dad?' I'd already opened a can and was heading through the shop to our house and my room. The ice-cool metal soothed my throbbing palm. My head felt like the big dipper. I couldn't figure out what had just happened and I didn't know what to do next. I needed time to think, alone. The last thing I wanted to do was chat with Dad.

'Cam, you all right, mate?'

'Yeah, Dad.' I kept walking, hoping he'd get the hint.

'You know you can always talk to me.' He stared, his eyes boring into me. 'Mate, your mother has been a bit tough on you lately and —'

That stopped me in my tracks. 'Lately?'

'Yeah, well, she has a lot going on. The move to the country's been hard for her. She's never lived anywhere but Beldare and she misses Grandma and Auntie Christine. It really hurt her to give up her job too …' Dad's voice trailed off. He stepped around from behind the counter and tossed me a King Rat, then picked up a licorice strap for himself. I chewed on the King Rat's head and peered at Dad. His eyes had the same look as Dracofir's when I'd left the cave. Maybe mine had the same pain in them and I'd never noticed. I decided I'd better check it out next time I looked in the mirror.

Much as I needed to think, Dad had me

interested. He'd never spoken to me about Mum like that. I dropped my backpack. My T-shirt sleeve flopped out through the open zip, thick mud and greenish sludge making the orange shirt look khaki.

'Dad, you know the stuff you said about Mum — well, I don't mean to be rude or anything, but it's been hard on us too, and we manage to be normal to each other.'

'So what do you call what you and Justin do to each other?' asked Dad with a grin, snapping off a piece of licorice.

'He's so perfect, Dad. Mum never screams at him.' I watched the bubbles pop along the rim of my drink can. 'She never calls him names or rolls her eyes when he drops a catch — oh, that's right, he doesn't drop them.'

'Don't blame Justin.' Dad sighed. 'I guess you should know, Cam. I'm sure you've heard us fighting …' Dad studied his licorice strap like his life depended on it. 'Cam, I was wrong not to talk to your mother or you boys about moving here, and I'm sorry. I should have asked you all how you felt, given you a chance to think about moving, instead of coming home and announcing I'd bought the shop. I just had to get away from the city after the bank thing.' He kept fiddling with the corner of his licorice strap.

'Do you mean the redundancy, Dad?'

'Yeah, mate, the redundancy. I thought a change of scenery would help. It hasn't worked out exactly as I'd planned. There's so much work, and financially the shop's in a worse state than I'd realised. Hopefully things'll look brighter after the accountant goes through the books tomorrow.' He leant across the counter and grabbed his cleaning spray. 'I guess, Cam, what I'm trying to say is — money is tight and Mum isn't happy.'

Wow! I felt so grown-up — special. No one, not even my teacher at Beldare, had spoken to me like that. I racked my brain for something to say — you know, something mature, comforting for Dad.

'Bummer, eh?' Not very mature or understanding, but it made Dad laugh. I tried again for a grown-up response. 'Dad, if we had more money, would things be better?'

'If we had more money, Cam, we could buy a home, rather than live behind the shop. Your mother could have her rose garden. You and Justin would have plenty of room to kick the footy. We could ditch that BMX once and for all and I'd buy you the cross-trainer you've been talking about. Hell, maybe I could buy myself one, too, and we could go for rides together.' Dad's eyes went all watery and floaty.

Warmth, as thick and golden as honey, spread down my shoulders into my arms, filling my chest and stomach. How good would it be to do stuff with Dad? We could be just like the fathers and sons you see on TV ads. An idea ballooned in the back of my head, filling my brain with endless possibilities. Why not? What did I have to lose?

'Thanks for the talk, Dad.' I drank the rest of my can, hiccuped and burped. 'Gotta go!' I grabbed my backpack and, as I slammed the door between our home and the shop, I heard Dad sigh, a leaden sigh that lasted for ages.

seven

Dear Cam,

Playing tennis at the lawn club. Back at 3.
Please finish your jobs and help Dad restock the shelves.
Love, Mum.

The note was scrawled in red pen on the back of an envelope.

I glanced around the kitchen. What a mess. Justin must have had scrambled eggs after I left. It looked like he'd scrambled the kitchen as well. I put in another load of laundry before tackling the mess.

While I worked, my brained sorted through information like a computer. I knew if we had more money Mum and Dad would be happier and life would be easier. And I knew Dracofir had the answer to our problems under her drag-egg. But I knew I couldn't steal from her. She would 'think' me coming, or whatever she does. Besides, stealing is wrong, I knew that. It doesn't matter who or what you steal from, it's still wrong.

I wiped up toast crumbs and swept the floor. As I reached for the dustpan, something clicked in the back of my mind. That was it! I could make life better and I didn't have to steal to do it!

Newspapers, magazines and television stations would pay squillions for proof that dragons existed! I'd sell Dracofir to one of them, or at least a photo of her, and I'd make a fortune!

I could buy an enormous house. Justin and I could have our own rooms. We could have a footy oval for Justin and a pool for me, maids and a cross-trainer, racer and mountain bike each. Dad could hire staff for the shop so he wouldn't have to work at all, and we could go for family bike rides and picnics and stuff. I'd make so much money, I'd even buy a holiday house at Seal Point.

And Mum would be happy. She'd have her rose garden, she could play tennis every day if she wanted to, and once a week she could dress up in her black dress, wear all her jewels and have drinks with her friends like she used to.

I could get a new dog, probably a Labrador, and I'd hire a personal trainer to teach me to kick a footy and catch a cricket ball.

I wiped the dishes, put the eggshells in the compost, refilled the washing machine and put the washing on the line, grinning all the time at my simple, yet clever plan.

But as I worked and schemed, something knocked at the back of my brain like a dripping tap. I tried to squash it by imagining a huge blue swimming pool — lap lane down one side, diving board at the house end, and spa at the other. An enormous blow-up lounge with a bright Hawaiian pattern floating in the centre of the pool.

Sunshine sparkled across the water making it glitter like one of Dracofir's diamonds. Dracofir!

Tap, tap, tap, tap. The thought drummed for my attention, changing from tap, tap, tap to tap-o-fir, tap-o-fir until it sounded like Dracofir, Dracofir, Dracofir. The more I tried to ignore it, the louder it became — so loud it made my forehead wrinkle. I scooped up the laundry basket and went inside for the next load.

Dracofir would probably be shut up in some cage and separated from her egg. People in white coats would prod her with needles and take her jewels. And I'd be proving her right, showing her my kind can't keep a promise.

But what did I care? She burnt my hand, threatened my life, breathed her stinky breath all over me, spat fire, hissed, laughed and yelled at me. It's not like she cared about me. And I didn't care about her.

But she had looked so sad and scared when I left.

Tough! She's a dragon — a fire-breathing, former people-eating, stealing dragon! At least, I figured she was a thief. All the stuff I read said dragons were dangerous thieves, so why would Dracofir be any different? Maybe she would come here and steal Mum's engagement ring. Boy, Mum would 'puffer fish' over that.

No, I had to do it, no matter how bad it made me feel. I had to sell Dracofir. She was the answer to my problems. Why else did I find her?

I grabbed a note pad and pen and parked myself by the kitchen phone. I had a clear view of the door to the shop so I could hang up straight away if Dad came my way.

I decided to start with Terry Tacker and Billy Burdock.

Last week I'd watched a TV show that called them 'media barons' and talked about how rich they were. The program talked about the film studios, television stations, newspapers and magazines they owned. I knew they'd be glad to get their hands on my dragon story. It would make more money for them and lots of money for me.

I phoned the telephone company for the numbers.

'Mr Tacker, please. Sydney, I think.'

'I need an initial and an address.'

'Terry — T. He's that really rich guy that owns everything.'

'I have no listing for a Reallyrichterrytacker.'

I screwed up my face and tried to think of the name of the family's company. 'Well, what about NEWS — that's News and Entertainment World Service?' I rapped the wall by the phone with my fingers, trying to tap louder than the thought of Dracofir that still beat in the back of my brain.

'NEWS, Sydney? Okay, please hold.' Finally a number! I stopped tapping and wrote down the number as the tin voice rattled it off. Instead of hanging up when the voice had finished, I held on for more information, just like the message said.

'What now? Billy Burdock?' Maybe this lady wasn't as slow as I thought.

'Yes please. World —'

'— wide Media, I know.' The tin voice spat out more numbers. This time I didn't hold for more information.

I tried Mr Burdock's office first.

'Worldwide Media. Good afternoon, this is Ellen.'

'Could I please speak to Mr Burdock?' I used my very best manners, the manners I use when I talk to Grandma.

'May I ask the nature of your business?'

'I have something he'll be very interested in.' I tried to sound grown-up and confident.

'Put it in writing, please. Good afternoon.' Beep, beep, beep. She hung up on me and my million, squillion dollar story! I 'ohed' and 'welled' like Mum for a moment before deciding Mr Burdock's loss was Mr Tacker's gain.

I stabbed the NEWS phone number into the keypad.

'News and Entertainment World Service. Good morning, this is Karen.' She sounded like a TV commercial for a bed shop.

'Good morning. I would like to speak to Mr Tacker.'

'Mr Tacker doesn't take outside calls. Would you care to leave a message with one of his secretaries?' invited the bed commercial. I hung up this time. They'd be crying when I signed film rights to an overseas company.

I couldn't reach the rich guys, so I changed to television. Downunder TV was first on my list.

'Hello. I would like to speak to the manager about a discovery I have made.' Again I tried the adult approach.

'A written request is required in the first instance.' She sounded just like all the other voices. I crossed Downunder TV off my list.

Eureka TV was next. This time I went with the direct approach.

'I have found a dragon and I want to talk to someone about it ... please.'

'Thanks for ringing, love, but see smallen don't smear swallegss.' At least, that's what I think she said. It was hard to tell because all her words ran together. Either she had some sort of speech problem or couldn't breathe very well. It almost sounded like she was laughing. I hung up on her too. I should have asked for her name so when I was rich and famous I could tell the story about the Eureka TV lady who laughed at my dragon.

Everybody knew the national networks had no money, so there was only one channel left — TV Today.

'Good morning, this is TVT. Chris speaking.'

'Hello. I have a dragon story to sell you.'

'A what?' It was hard to tell if this person was a man or a woman, but whatever it was, it was very rude.

'A dragon story.'

'This is a ridiculous way to spend your holidays. I'm having a bad day and you're making it worse. Go play in the fresh air or something.'

I'm glad I didn't tell it my name, because I got kind of rude back. 'Shove the phone up your bum!' I yelled, then hung up — again.

I wished I'd never messed with TV. I sat perched on the kitchen table for ages, terrified TV Today might have put a trace on me, like the police do in movies.

After half-an-hour, when police dressed in thick black vests, pointing even blacker guns, hadn't burst through the back door to drag me off to jail, I went back to the shop and helped Dad stack shelves. We didn't talk much because Dad had to keep zipping back to the counter to serve customers. The time alone gave me the chance to organise my next attack.

Most of my 'planning time' was spent telling myself I was doing the right thing. I even had myself believing that if I told the world about Dracofir, she would be happy to help people with all sorts of problems and answer those questions no one ever can — you know, like why dogs eat their sick, why spiders always charge at the person who is most frightened of them and why holidays go faster than school days. Maybe she knew how to cure cancer. Selling Dracofir would help me and the rest of the world also.

Well, if wealthy men and television stations weren't interested in my story, maybe radio would be. But which station should I try? Thoughts spun around my brain like out-of-control dodgem cars. Some crashed before they even started moving, while others managed a few laps before charging headfirst into another. My brain sparked and whirred while I dusted and packed.

I could try a talk-station like the one Mum listened to. The announcer had a booming voice as thick as honey and as sour as lemon. He talked about anything... families, politics, road-rage, even schools, but he didn't have much time for kids, and he certainly didn't give away heaps of money.

There was the local station, Wilton Gold. A dragon living next to Lake Warrong would shove the footy and cricket aside for a bit. But the local station was hard up for money — all the competitions had scabby prizes, like CD singles, packets of chips, vouchers to Chicken Chow or tickets to the local cinema. None of these were what I was after.

Then again, I could try ERA FM, the music station I used to listen to in Beldare. ERA FM was dead cool. They gave away stacks of prizes. You could win concert tickets with backstage passes or a thousand dollars just for a joke. And they gave away cars. Any place that could give away cars had to be made of money.

That was my choice. ERA FM.

eight

My fingers thumped Dad's bedside table in time with the ringing of the phone. I was a jolting mass of nerves.

I'd sneaked out of the shop when Mr Logan, or Knacka, arrived. Mr Logan got his nickname because of his old business. He used to own 'Logan's Knackery' but had to sell after the accident. Dad told me the kid working for Knacka didn't tie a dead bull onto the truck properly. Knacka was standing beside the truck, talking to the farmer, when the kid jumped into the cabin and turned the key. The truck kangaroo-hopped and the dead bull rolled off the tray, landing on Knacka. Since the accident, the toes on Knacka's left foot point to the right and he has to use a walking stick. 'Did me back in,' he says. He sold the business and retired. He comes in every day for his bread and milk and three chocolate frogs. Knacka stays for ages, telling stories about bloated cattle, rotting horses and eyeless sheep. It's too much for me. Makes my stomach heave. If I had a choice between Knacka and Pucker, I'd take Pucker every time. Better a wobbly bum and a lipstick-stained dog than a blood-stained hat and bloodthirsty chat.

At the sight of Knacka's old, stained hat bobbing past the window, I bolted for Mum and Dad's room to use the phone.

My parents' room was at the other end of the house so Dad couldn't hear me from the shop and, even if he came this way, every floorboard would groan a warning. Our house talks more than Pucker and Knacka combined.

My fingers drummed, the phone brrr-brrred and my heart thudded, threatening to leap out of my mouth and burst on Mum's cream quilt cover.

'Only the Best, ERA FM. This is Ledge.'

My heart beat faster. A drought settled in my mouth and my tongue swelled until it stuck like prawn crackers to the roof of my mouth. I hadn't dreamt Ledge would answer his own phone.

I picked Ledge, the afternoon announcer on ERA FM, because he was so cool. He played great music and hung out with bands, singers and actors. I also chose him because he gave himself the nickname Ledge. He believes he's a legend, or at least that's what people say. With an ego like that, I thought he'd go sick over my dragon story. He'd have it in every newspaper and magazine and he'd take me on TV talk shows with him. Maybe Dracofir would come with us and be interviewed, too.

This was it. This was my chance to talk to Ledge, make heaps of money and solve my family's problems all at once.

'H-h-h-helloth, Ledgeth.' Half of my brain groaned, the other half was grateful I'd phoned instead of facing him with my story. I would have collapsed.

'What's your request, kid?' His voice was a wall of noise, even deeper and smoother than on the radio. My heart dropped from my mouth to my stomach and fluttered around like a trapped moth. I made swishy noises in the back of my throat, trying to get some spit happening so I could loosen my tongue.

'No. No, n-not a —'

'Hey, kid, spit it out or get off the phone!' I could almost see his eyes roll. I took a deep breath and did what I do when I go swimming, I dived straight in.

'Mr Ledge, I have something to tell you that will amaze you.' I sounded like a salesman — almost.

'Go on.' I could hear music and the click of a keyboard.

'For the right price —' I'd watched enough movies to know the talk '— I'll tell you about — no, *show* you — the most incredible creature you'll ever see.'

'I'm listening…'

'I can show you a dragon and a cave full of every treasure you can imagine. There's an egg too. The dragon has a really bad temper. When she gets mad she kind of hisses like a snake, like this: ssss.' I paused, partly for a breath and partly because I thought I could hear rumbling.

It wasn't Dad. I'd only left the shop fifteen minutes ago, so it was a dead cert. Knacka would still be there, leaning on the counter, lifting his hat to scratch his head and filling Dad with dead-animal horror stories.

It wasn't thunder. Outside, the sky was like a picture in a travel brochure advertising dream holidays in places that never rain.

A snort? Did I hear a snort? The rumble was laughter rolling out of the phone. Burning embarrassment crawled up my chest.

'Go on, kid, this is great.' Ledge's laughter was as thick and deep as his voice. 'I'll just get set to record this, eh?'

'Mr Ledge, this isn't a joke. I have seen a dragon and have a burn on my palm to prove it.' I opened my hand. Earlier today the burn had been blistered and weeping clear gunk. Now it was gone. My palm was pink and criss-crossed with its usual lines. The only mark was under my little finger; a small scar from when I cut my hand on a drink can at the Melbourne Show.

It didn't make any sense. My palm had throbbed earlier in the day, but now the pain was gone. I prodded it with my finger. It felt perfectly normal. I had nothing — no blister, scar or even pain to prove Dracofir had burnt me.

'The dragon's name is D-D-D-Dracofir.' I stumbled over her name, my voice a whisper.

'Okay, I'm all set, kid. Tell me your joke again.'

'I'm not joking.'

Ledge roared with laughter. I even thought I heard him slap the desk. 'You crack me up, kid. Now cut the crap. Either you tell me this joke or you get off my phone.'

'I'm not telling you anything till I get paid.'

'Stuff that, kid! Stop wasting my time. Loser!' He slammed the phone down so hard it made me jump. My face burnt and tears welled in my eyes, making everything do a rainbow dance.

He laughed at me. Ledge. Ledge, the Legend of Radio, the man who hung out with the coolest bands and was photographed with TV stars, called me a loser. Ledge thought I was a loser.

I placed the phone back in its cradle, frightened it might explode like a grenade. I stepped off Mum and Dad's bed and smoothed the crinkled quilt cover. I swallowed and sniffed away my tears as I dragged myself down the hall to my room. I eased the door open, then threw myself on the bed. I lay staring at the ceiling, not making a sound. I was too sad and too embarrassed to cry out loud. My heart ached like my legs after a long run and my chest felt as if it would burst and splatter the walls.

Maybe I'd die of embarrassment.

Mum, Dracofir, Ledge, the kids at school, even Justin — they all laughed at me. I hated that sound. It roared and crashed in your head like a breaking wave, and stabbed your heart with blunt fingers.

I was only trying to help. I had to stop Mum and Dad from getting a divorce, because that's what happens. Tommy Jenkins told me. Tommy was in my grade at St Anne's in Beldare. His parents got divorced.

During the school walkathon Tommy told me what happened. He and I talked more than walked. We talked about Nintendo, Pokémon, Mrs Grove's hairy chin and divorce. Tommy said he couldn't remember his parents ever being happy. He said they fought about money all the time. I saw tears trickle down his face, but pretended I hadn't noticed. We weren't the type of friends who could bawl in front of each other. Anyway that's how I knew. That's how I knew parents divorce over money, and getting money for Dracofir was my way of stopping the divorce and making our life happy again.

And I'd blown it.

I sat up and shook my head. My room felt strange — darker, yet the sun still streamed through the window, spilling golden light over the flowery floor and my blue and yellow doona. I looked around ... the posters of Ian Thorpe and *Star Wars* all looked normal. The line of toilet paper lay undisturbed, dividing my half of the room from Justin's. Even his neat half looked normal.

But somehow it felt different, colder, like I wasn't alone.

Perhaps this was how it felt before your chest burst and splattered blood and guts everywhere. I rubbed my chest and blew my nose.

That smell! What was it? I breathed deeply. Meat ... roast meat ... no, ice-cream, or was it ice?

Dracofir!

My heart's ache was squashed by pounding fear.

She'd told me dragons had special ways. She could understand my thoughts and could change size — it was only a couple of hours since I'd seen her shrink from the size of an elephant to that of a Great Dane. Maybe she could become invisible too. Maybe she was perched on Justin's bed, waiting to pounce.

I should never have tried to sell her. I broke my promise. I had proved I was no better than the other people Dracofir hated.

I leapt off the bed and ran screaming to the shop. I didn't care if Knacka, Pucker, Mum, Matt, Josh and all the West boys were in there.

'Dad! Dad!' Wheeze. Pant. Puff. 'Dad!'

No Knacka, no Pucker, no Mum, no Matt, no Josh and no West boys — just Emily Griffith, a Grade 6 girl at my school, St Augustine's.

Dad and Emily stared at me, frozen, hands outstretched to give and receive money. I skidded to a halt like Coyote in Road Runner cartoons. I'm sure, if I'd looked, I would have seen little puffs of smoke coming from my heels.

'What's wrong, Cameron?' Dad usually called me Cam or mate, or buddy when he'd been to the footy with his friends. He saved 'Cameron' for when I was in trouble.

Think! I couldn't tell him there was a dragon in my bedroom — certainly not in front of Emily

Griffith. If *she* laughed at me too, my chest would definitely burst open.

'Hello, Emily.' I smiled one of those smiles that's so pathetic you want to run and hide before you finish making it.

'Hi.' She didn't take her wide, twinkling eyes off me. This would have to be good.

'What's up, Cameron?' Dad's eyes were no longer wide and they sure didn't twinkle.

'Finish with Emily, Dad. It can wait.' I joined my hands in front of me and watched my thumbs do that little dance — the 'I'm just standing here minding my own business' dance.

'Glory, Cam, it can't be nothing. You charged in here like a steam train and made twice as much noise.'

'Well, it's just …' My brain was like the first page of a new exercise book — blank. 'Well, you see, Dad …'

'Spit it out, Cameron.'

'I left my jumper down by the lake.'

'Is that it? All that bellowing over a jumper?' Dad shook his head. 'Why you'd need a jumper today, I'll never know. It's as hot as hell.'

Emily gathered her newspaper and carton of milk and strolled out of the shop. 'Goodbye, Mr Mason. See ya!'

I'm sure she was laughing.

'Bye, Emily!' Dad called after her. 'Well, mate, you'd better get it, or your mother will really give you a reason to bellow.'

'Yeah, I'm on my way.' But I wasn't. The front page headline of the *Wilton Times* fixed my feet to the spot: 'LAKE DEVELOPMENT ALL SET TO START'.

I lunged forward and grabbed the paper, scanning it for details.

'Three days,' I groaned.

'Cam, what is going on? You charged in here like your bum was on fire and now you're reading the paper, calm as you like.' Dad stood behind the counter, watching me with narrowed eyes.

'Do you know much about the lake development, Dad?'

'Only what's been in the paper the last couple of months. Why?'

'I was wondering what was going to happen.'

Fear resurfaced in my belly — not fear for me but fear for Dracofir.

'The council and some city businessman are redeveloping the lake's north shore. They'll tear down the trees, rip up the old drains and build a motel. Should be very flash — five-star, according to the paper.' Dad grabbed a box of cellophane bags and started filling them with lollies. 'Good for business, I'd say.'

'So the drains will be ripped up?'

'Apparently so.'

'And the bush and stuff removed?'

'Yep. Was that fifty or sixty jelly babies? They'll make it into a flash beach and recreation spot.'

'But why will they redevelop the drains?'

'Blast! How many jelly babies did I count into this damn thing? Cam, why the sudden interest in drains?' Dad glared.

'It's just I've met this ... ah ... friend and she's lived under ... on the north shore of the lake for years. What'll happen to her, Dad?'

'Does she live in one of those shacks overlooking the lake?'

I nodded.

'I thought the council moved everyone out.' Dad went back to counting. 'They're going to pull down those houses and rip up the hill.'

I thought my knees would crumple. I tossed the paper towards the pile and bolted for the door.

'Cameron, for heaven's sake! The paper!'

The toss had been a little firmer than I'd meant. The pages scattered and fluttered to the floor like autumn leaves in the wind.

'Sorry, Dad. I'll pay for it when I get back.'

'And find that jumper!'

nine

Dracofir's cave was empty when I returned. Empty and silent, like a library and filled with just as many stories and secrets.

The nest and floor were as I'd last seen them, but the drag-egg had changed slightly. Its colours were more vibrant and sparkled like dewdrops in the morning sun. The lines were harder to see. They were melting into each other, joining to make one new, brighter colour.

'Dracofir!' My voice bounded around the

cave, each echo chasing the others. 'It's me, Cam. I need to talk to you.'

Silence battered my ears. Ignoring the crunching and popping beneath my feet, I tiptoed around the cave, calling, and searching for her in every rock face and lump in the floor. I thought about approaching her precious egg — it flushed her out last time.

'Dracofir, please. You and your egg are in danger.'

'*Drag*-egg! How many times do I have to tell you?'

I spun around, searching the cave for her.

'Up here, Cameron.' Her voice was quiet and low — mellow is the word, I think. I looked to the skylight. Dracofir was perched on a rock, staring down at me with the same quizzical look as a cockatoo in a cage. She stretched her wings and glided to the cave floor, growing to what I guessed was her real dragon size, about as large as an elephant.

'What brings you back, man-boy?' Dracofir landed on the floor at my feet.

My lurching stomach seemed to have

swallowed my voice. What if she knew I'd tried to tell people about her? What if she knew I tried to sell her? Would she rip me apart with those huge claws, then eat me, or roast me first with her flames, then eat me? I decided not to mention the whole selling thing for now and hope she hadn't 'thought' it already. I was more worried about the lake development and the danger that lay ahead for Dracofir and her drag-egg.

'I ... Dracofir, you and your egg — your drag-egg, are in danger.' My voice returned, but it ran away without me. 'The council and some rich guy are going to rip up the hill and the drain. You have to leave. They'll find you and hurt you.'

'Why does that concern you, Cameron-duncanmason?' Her eyes, as deep and still as the lake itself, seemed to look right into my heart.

'They'll hurt you. The hill will be ripped up. It might collapse and kill you and your drag-egg. And what if they find you and trap you?'

Dracofir snorted and huffed. 'Again, why is it your concern?' She brought her face close to mine.

'It'd be awful.' I wanted to tell her I liked coming to visit, that I enjoyed her stories and wanted to learn more. I tried to tell her I'd like to help with the drag-egg and that I wanted to be her friend, but my voice stuck in my throat. Instead I reached out with trembling fingers and touched her jaw.

I'd expected her to feel rough and cold like old leather gardening boots, but she felt warm and soft, her skin as smooth as mine. I looked into her huge eyes. The ground seemed to become soft, like mud, and the air warm and soothing. In a slow movement I withdrew my hand, but held Dracofir's gaze.

'Cameronduncanmason, it is no different from what people have done time and time again. I have known of the approach of this storm for some time, but I miscalculated its arrival. I believed I had time to create a nest, lay my drag-egg and see it hatch and grow before I had to leave. It seems this may not be.' Dracofir pushed a huge blue piece of plastic with her foot. 'You see, Cameronduncanmason, the drag-egg cannot be disturbed until it has hatched, and I must remain with it until it hatches — no matter the cost.'

'You can't, Dracofir. If they find you and your egg, they'll lock you away.'

'Yes, man-boy, that is your nature.'

'I don't understand, Dracofir. What is our nature?'

'Look into my eyes, Cameronduncanmason.'

A huge glistening tear welled in Dracofir's eye. It swelled and rolled like a bubble to the edge, balancing perfectly in the corner.

'Watch carefully, man-boy, and I will show you.'

Silence roared in my ears. I felt strange, my head all fuzzy as if I was on a fast merry-go-round. I could hear Dracofir's voice, but not in my ears. It was inside my head, as if I was thinking it.

As I watched, the tear changed from silver to a mixture of colours. My ankles became rubbery and I grew light, like froth on the top of a milk-shake. I was being drawn inside the tear of amazing colours. I chewed my bottom lip and clenched my fists.

A cool breeze caressed my face. Goose bumps popped up on my arms and legs. I opened one eye, then the other. Dracofir and the cave had disappeared. I stood on the edge of a high cliff, looking down on a huge green forest.

Trees reached so high they poked holes in the sky. Polished water trickled in the rivers and streams, winding its way through valleys and over plains. Birds sang. Animals — lions, tigers, elephants, giraffes, deer: every animal I'd ever heard of and more — slept, prowled and preened. Exquisite perfumed flowers bloomed everywhere.

I breathed deeply. I'd never smelt or seen anything so pure. I had to be a part of this. I searched the cliff face for a path down, only to see the forest scene shunt forward, to be replaced by other scenes, each rolling past like a slow train.

People dressed in skins and coloured cloth worked and sang outside dried-grass huts. The scene shunted forward and instead of huts, pressed-earth houses and people in flowing robes appeared before me.

Men trapped animals, felled trees and built

houses. Clearings spread before my eyes, eating the forest. Humans on horses galloped after deer. Men dressed in armour poured into villages, set them alight, then left, dragging their loot behind them.

American buffalo munched on crisp grass, only to be mown down by rifle fire. The once-green grass, heavy with dew, was bathed in blood.

Wounded whales were dragged behind boats. Gorillas, rhinoceros, tigers and elephants lay in pools of blood, missing parts of their bodies and left for vultures.

Deep pits gaped in green hills; cement, brick and wooden buildings replaced pressed earth and logs; taller and taller structures appeared. Trucks spewed garbage into wide holes. Mounds of twisted plastic flapped in the breeze. Cars, trucks and factories belched fumes into the air. Cracked pools of mud replaced clear streams. Animals fled from the water, but others, desperate to drink, dropped on the banks.

Stomping feet announced the arrival of armies. Screams filled the air, drowning out the thud of bombs. A bright flash filled the sky and a pinky-grey mushroom cloud swallowed it.

'What are we doing?' I whispered. The pink and grey cloud blurred. Colours merged into a silver swirl. I blinked and again I stood in front of Dracofir, staring into her tear. The tear spilt forward and splashed onto the cave floor.

No wonder she hated us. No wonder she hated me. Wait till she found out I had tried to betray her. My knees buckled and I crumpled to the floor like a cloth doll.

'Sssseee what humansss have done, sss Cameronduncanmason? What a messss you have made. Ssssome of it is of ussse, I grant you, but at what cossst to other creaturesss? In creating a better world for yourssselvesss, you have ruined the earth for ssso many othersss. You humansss have no regard for anything but yourselvesss.'

'Not all of us. Some of us try.' It sounded pathetic, but I had to say something.

'Do they, man-boy? Look at what isss planned for the lake. Will it serve the earth better? A cement monstrosssity replacing treesss, grassesss and shrubsss. And what will happen to the possums, the water rats, the pelicans and the fish sss? Greed. Never has there been a greedier creature.'

I looked at my feet, ashamed of myself and my race. Dracofir's jewels danced in my mind.

'Look at your treasure,' I pointed, 'and your cave floor. Isn't that greed?'

'What you see, Cameronduncanmason, has been gathered by my parents, grandparents and their parents. Dragons once mixed freely with people. You needed us. We protected your flocks from trolls, your wealth from bandits, your kingdoms from invaders — and you paid us handsomely.' She paced as she spoke, stretching her wings and shaking her head. 'Then people became greedy and wanted the treasures back. We were painted as evil and grasping, vengeful, cunning, bad-tempered, and terrifying — wasn't that what your precious Internet showed you?' She stopped and frowned at me. 'People slaughtered us until only a few remained. The lies ...' She settled a scale that threatened to fall from her left leg and snapped her face to mine. 'Only then did we begin stealing ... but we stole back what was ours. Don't believe everything you read about us, Cameron-duncanmason.'

For the first time since she had begun speaking, Dracofir settled on the floor. She crossed her front legs in front of her and closed her eyes.

Silence hung in the air. I couldn't read her mood. I waited for her to speak first.

After a few slow and silent minutes Dracofir opened her eyes. 'Do you have questions, man-boy?'

'Why did you come here, Dracofir?'

Her eyes twinkled and she peeled her lips back from her teeth. 'I am here because the Drakensberg Dragon Council sent me. My quest was to find a safe environment, a home where dragons could drink pure water, live in dry caves and eat our fill of grass-fed bullocks and lamb. A place where we could protect our world and be left alone. A place that was near a Spring of Life. I thought I had found it. I thought I'd found a good place ...'

'For what?'

'For us to live, undisturbed. A place where we could care for our young and the environment. A place where we could continue to be the Keepers of the Earth.' She puffed out her chest. 'Self-appointed, I grant you, but we take our role seriously.'

More questions burst into my head. 'How long have you been here?'

'At Lake Warrong, over twenty years. No one suspected I was here, but then I sensed the storm, and I knew I needed help.' Dracofir flicked her head at the coloured egg. 'I laid it five human years ago. It is due to hatch any day and until it does I am stranded — tied to the cave. Even then I cannot move the dragling unless I have a specially prepared cave. I need to find us a new home.'

'Is that why you watched me? So I could help you?'

'I have watched many man-boys and woman-girls, but I chose you as the one. You had no friends and you fought with your family, so I knew there was no one you would tell of my existence.'

No one to tell! My face burned. I stared at my knees and fiddled with a piece of pink plastic.

'I was aware of your family's unhappiness and knew trusting you would be a gamble, but I could see no other way. I let you find me. I allowed you into my home where no other human has been.'

I could feel her staring at me. I raised my head. 'Dracofir, I'd like to stay with your egg and protect it while you search for a safer home.'

She did that leering, drooling thing again. Her eyes brightened and twinkled. 'I believe you mean that, man-boy.'

'I do. Please, let me show you I'm different.'

'What if you get a better offer? How do I know you won't steal my jewels and sell my dragegg?' Dracofir furrowed her brow and pushed her face closer to mine. It was as though she was looking into my heart for the answer.

Panic raced through my body. I was as greedy as every other human she'd spoken about. I wished she would eat me. 'Dracofir, I tried to tell people about you and get money for the story so I could make my family happy again. But I was wrong. I knew it even when I was speaking to Ledge.' I buried my face between my knees. 'Just eat me,' I whispered.

A snorting, growling noise filled the air. 'You did not do a very good job though.'

'You already knew, didn't you?'

'I hoped you would tell me yourself, and you have.'

'I'm glad it didn't work. I don't know what I was thinking. I guess I was angry.' I looked up into her face. 'Dracofir, I am truly sorry. I'd never have forgiven myself if my plan had worked.'

'I thought it an unusual action for you, Cameronduncanmason. Where did you tell that person to put their phone?'

'It's not funny, Dracofir; I nearly did a terrible thing.' I stood and stepped towards her. 'I mean it, I am more sorry than I've ever been in my life. Please believe me. I really do want to help you.'

With a shimmer of her scales and a lash of her tail, Dracofir began pacing again — five steps forward, five steps back — muttering and hissing under her breath. Huge globs of foaming spit fell from her mouth. Her tail swished past my face, blasting icy air and the smell of roasting meat around me. 'We need to eat, to hunt. I can't leave the drag-egg — not with this going on. I need to explore the rainforest.' She froze in her tracks and shook her head from side to side. 'What would Drashini do?' Her once thundering voice was barely a whisper.

'Dracofir,' I kept my voice as low as hers, 'Who is Drashini?'

Dracofir pushed out her chest. Light flashed in her eyes. 'Drashini, Cameronduncanmason, is the leader of the Drakensberg Dragon Council, leader of all dragons, adviser to the Fairy Kingdom.' She snorted. 'Yes, boy, fairies exist. Don't give me that look.' She studied her drag-egg before continuing.

'Drashini is our leader, like your prime minister. She is one of the oldest surviving dragons. Some say she is over five hundred years old; others say she is closer to six hundred. She is the wisest of our kind. She forged deals with knights bent on destroying us, saved the Curlivoxes, Keepers of the Forests, from extinction at the hands of the dull-witted Trolls, and it's even been whispered she created the potion that eliminated the Black Death in the Middle Ages.' Dracofir settled into a sitting position, paws crossed in front of her like an obedient dog.

'Drashini chose my mate Smaufir for me, and fifty years ago sent us to the Southern Hemisphere — Smaufir to New Zealand to search the mountains and lakes for a home, and me to Australia to hatch our dragling and widen the search.'

'Lake Warrong is a funny place to settle. Dad dragged us here reluctantly, yet you chose it. Seems like a weird choice to me.'

'It has been perfect until now. Lake Warrong is close to food and is only a short flight from the ocean and the Geonite Rainforest. You see, there is an ancient Spring of Life deep within the rainforest. This spring still runs free and clean, thanks to my vigilance. Lake Warrong is fed by the spring, as is the Geonite River which runs through the rainforest.' A tiny puff of smoke shot out of her nostrils, and her lips curled. 'As I told you, if the spring is blocked, our earth cannot renew. There can be no seasons, no growth.'

It still seemed a strange place to settle. Dracofir had the whole of Australia to choose from ... the Dandenongs, the Blue Mountains, even that place I did a project on last year — the Hinterland in Queensland. Surely there were ancient springs there too. Why here?

Dracofir dropped her head on her crossed legs, then whispered, 'There is a magical history to the place, and there are fewer people here than in those other areas you considered.'

'How do you do that?' I spluttered. 'I only thought about those places. I didn't say a word!'

More puffs of smoke and curling lips and even a little sigh. 'Man-boy, it is too complex for a human brain to absorb, but yes, I can feel what you are thinking.'

'Even when I am at home?' My hand flew to my mouth, trying to shove the words back.

'Yes, even at home.' She frowned. 'Cam, your

mother has finished her tennis, and you have not finished your jobs — stacking the shelves, remember?'

'Incredible. Teach me how to do it! Please!'

'I cannot. Unlike humans with your five senses, dragons have nine. They cannot be taught, only improved.'

'Nine senses? What are they?'

Dracofir sighed. 'They are similar to human senses, but stronger. We have a sense of smell like you, only heightened. We smell not just odours, but also emotions like fear and love. We can smell lies, illness and impending death. We have excellent vision and very sensitive hearing, far superior to any other creature. Our sense of taste is duller than yours, mainly due to the gases which create our fire and smoke. See how they have seared my mouth?' She opened her mouth and I leant inside. Behind the red gums and pools of spit I could see charcoal-like black marks. The stench was overpowering. I stepped back and sucked in fresh air through my mouth, hoping she didn't think me rude. I wondered if she could smell her own breath, but she started on her sense of touch before I could ask.

'Our touch, too, is dull, yet my nose and belly are extremely sensitive. I can feel a tree grow simply by pressing my nose or belly to the earth. The rest of me does not have this power.'

'That's five, Dracofir. What are the others?'

'Our sixth sense is what you would call ESP or mind reading, only far more involved. We are able to feel and understand the thoughts of all life on earth, and linked to this is our seventh sense — our ability to understand the languages of all species and subspecies as soon as we are born. Not only do we understand, but we can communicate with these creatures. Our communication sense is such we have no need for phones or faxes or e-mail. If Drashini calls a meeting of the DDC I am able to attend, simply by tuning in. And that is our eighth sense.' She stopped and did one of her snarling grin things. 'Amazing, isn't it?'

'And the ninth?'

'We are magic creatures — not like your

human magicians who pull rabbits from hats, but truly magic.'

'That's why you can change shape?'

'Yes, but that is only a small part of my skill. Cameronduncanmason, my sixth sense tells me your mother has just finished her second cup of tea. Surely she cannot drink a third. Go now. Your jobs await you.'

'Can I come back tomorrow, please?'

'Early.'

ten

I thought Mum fussed when she hired a new baby-sitter, but Dracofir was even worse. I'd already repeated her instructions twice, and that was after she'd explained them four times. I was about to tell her that even though I only had five senses, I was quite able to follow directions, when her steely voice broke into my thoughts.

'Do you understand, Cameronduncan-mason?'

'Yes, Dracofir, I've got it.'

'Tell me once again so I can be sure.'

I sighed and started to repeat her list of dos and don'ts. 'I'm to stay out of the inner two rings of the nest —'

'Which are they?'

'The yellow one filled with blankets and lambskins —'

'And?'

'The middle one filled with jewels, the centre of the nest where the drag-egg lies.'

'Why?'

'Because if I enter these rings I will disturb the hatching rhythms. The nest pattern corresponds to the drag-egg pattern. If the nest is disturbed it will affect the dragling's development. Any interference will disrupt the rhythms and kill the dragling.' I rattled off the explanation with as much enthusiasm as I recite my times-tables. The explanation had been fascinating at first, but after an hour of listening to a ranting, panicky dragon, the story had lost its appeal.

'Good, good. And if the drag-egg wobbles or changes colour to fresh strawberry red?'

'I bash the skylight with this drumstick.' I twirled the piece of wood Dracofir called 'the Fafnor' in the air. About a metre long, the branch appeared to be covered in tiny carvings, but when I picked it up I could see they were tiny paintings of dragons, fairies, kings, knights and drag-eggs.

'Cameronduncanmason, the Fafnor is no laughing matter.' She used the voice that made me feel really dumb. 'Elder-mother gave me the Fafnor and it was given to her by her elder-mother. The drawings show the history of my family. See at the bottom, beneath the one-eyed troll, that is me as I hatched.'

I studied the stick. Peeking out from a cracked drag-egg shell was a miniature version of Dracofir. She looked exactly as she did today, only much smaller. 'Wow! You haven't changed a bit.'

Dracofir ignored me. 'The Fafnor is the link between a dragling and its mother. When you knock on the Eye of the Sky three times, the vibrations will reach me no matter where I am. Perhaps this isssn't sssuch —'

'Dracofir, I'm sorry, I was teasing. If the drag-egg wobbles it is about to hatch and I must bang the Fafnor on the Eye of the Sky three times, but if the drag-egg turns strawberry red, it's an emergency and I have to bang five times. See? I did listen. I'll take fantastic care of your drag-egg, I promise. It's just, well — you're worse than Auntie Christine. Mum and I looked after my cousin when he was two months old and you should have heard Auntie Christine go on before she left. Mum said she was a neuro, neurtic — no, neurotic mother.'

'I'm sorry, Cameronduncanmason. Five years is a long time to wait. My last dragling didn't survive the hatching …' Her mouth twitched and a shadow clouded her eyes.

'Dracofir, couldn't you just read my mind and know if there was a problem?'

'I am unable to search and also keep a constant link to your thoughts, man-boy. The Fafnor is far more reliable. But if you think you are unable —'

'If anything, anything at all changes, even

the wind, I'll tap the Eye of the Sky three times with the Fafnor, I promise.

'You are a good boy, man-boy, better than most. I will return before the longest shadows cross the Eye of the Sky.'

She disappeared before she'd finished speaking, leaving me alone in her home. At first I stood at the cave entrance like the guard outside Buckingham Palace. Then I tried to memorise the layers of the nest. I cleaned my nails with my pocket knife and scratched the dirt from the ripples in the soles of my sneakers — and that was the first half-hour gone. I'd never been so bored. And hungry! I cut a couple of laps around the cave looking for something to eat — anything, but I could only find a couple of bleached bones.

I decided with Dracofir gone it was the perfect chance to explore. I don't know what I'd hoped to find — more treasure, Dracofir's bed, a magical book, even a discarded scale — but in my search and endless laps of the cave, I found nothing. I even tried to climb the back wall to reach her high perch, but fell before I'd made it five centimetres off the ground. I rubbed my bottom and retreated to the cave entrance. Apart from the nest, drag-egg, and the Eye of the Sky, there was nothing unusual about the cave. Disappointed, I slumped to the floor and waited for Dracofir's return.

By the time she returned to the dark and silent cave, I was a gasp away from madness and a rumble from starvation.

'How'd it go? Did you find a good spot? Did you look in the rainforest or go to the cliffs by the beach?' I bounced questions at Dracofir as she hovered above her nest, then landed at the back of the cave. She shook her wings and folded them before settling on the cave floor.

'Come back tomorrow,' she said and closed her eyes.

I was stunned. After I'd spent the day, bored stupid, staring at her sparkling egg, I was being dismissed. I gathered my backpack and headed for the tunnel, my mind blank.

'Be here early, Cameronduncanmason,' she called as I crawled out into the drain.

I rode home slowly to conserve my energy — I needed food.

• • •

The next day I took survival rations — a salad roll, two apples, a large packet of nacho-flavoured corn chips, four Rainbow Pythons, a two-litre bottle of lemonade and a family block of peppermint chocolate. I sneaked Justin's colour GameBoy from his bedside table, the book Mrs Samson recommended as holiday reading: *A Wrinkle in Time*, and three Batman comics from the shop. I even packed pencils and paper so I could try to sketch the cave and nest. Boy, it was hard to lug my backpack all the way to the cave. It was too full to wear in the tunnel, so I had to push it ahead of me.

Dracofir left without uttering four words and by the time she returned, I was down to my last apple. She appeared in a blast of wind and shook herself in the cave entrance, growing to her normal size with each shake. I raced forward to meet her, hoping she'd be more chatty than she had been yesterday and this morning.

Again she hovered over her nest, inspecting her drag-egg, then landed at the back of the cave. She rattled and stomped, then flopped on her stomach, acting as though I didn't exist.

I tried a friendlier approach. 'Welcome back, Dracofir. Nothing to report here. Your drag-egg has been beautifully behaved. How was the house hunting?'

'Good,' she huffed, looking around the cave. Her gaze stopped at where I had spent the day eating, reading, drawing and playing GameBoy. Crumpled paper and empty packets lay scattered across the cave floor.

'I didn't mean to make such a mess. I'll clean it up.' I rushed forward, scooped up my things and shoved them in the backpack.

'Go home, Cameronduncanmason. Clean it up and go.'

• • •

On the way home my mind whirred in circles like my bike wheels. Feelings of anger, excitement, frustration and hope spun around and around. Part of me was angry at Dracofir for being so rude and ungrateful. I couldn't help wondering why I was wasting my time with her and I seriously toyed with the idea of not going back, but I knew in my heart I had to. I had to for two reasons: one was I'd promised and the most important one was I was excited — excited that Dracofir trusted me with her drag-egg; excited to be part of this magic; and excited to have a friend. I was hooked on the magic and hooked on Dracofir. I liked her, in spite of her moods, and I loved her stories. Dragons, fairies, trolls and magic — wasn't that enough to be excited about? And she had a great sense of humour for a grumpy dragon. Much as she frustrated me with her rudeness at times, I knew I'd be heading back tomorrow.

I could handle Dracofir's silences okay, but hanging around the cave all day made it pretty tough to get my jobs done. I had to be up by six-thirty, showered by seven, have the washing machine on by ten past seven and the vacuuming done by seven-thirty to have any chance of getting to Dracofir by eight-thirty. It was tough sticking to my timetable with the family's complaints about noise. I tried explaining to Mum and Justin that the vacuuming had to be done, but they couldn't be convinced. And when I suggested to Mum that maybe I didn't need to vacuum every day because she never used to, she did the puffer-fish thing and I had to bolt into the shop to escape — straight into the dog-kissing lips of Pucker.

Dad didn't mind the noise, but then again, he started work in the shop at six.

When I got home after a day in the cave, drag-egg-sitting, I had to race around bringing in laundry, and then help cook tea and do the dishes. Between dragons, puffer fish and enough jobs to punish a murderer, I was stuffed.

And was anyone grateful? Dracofir was in a foul mood and barely spoke, Mum puffed and raved about noise and lack of sleep, and Justin complained about my side of our room.

Life sure was hard work.

With a full and heavy backpack, I returned to the cave for day three of egg-sitting.

I discovered Dracofir's temper had improved little.

'Good morning, Cameronduncanmason. I will be late today. I shall return after the long shadows have settled for the evening.' She flapped her wings, rose into the air and disappeared.

'So how will I get the laundry in tonight?' I called after her shadow. I shook my head and trudged to my spot by the cave entrance.

•••

Six-thirty pm and no sign of Dracofir. I'd slept-in that morning and hadn't had time to start my jobs before I left, so I knew I was in for a major pufferfish attack when I got home. The later it became, the greater the attack would be.

'Cameronduncanmason!' Dracofir's voice boomed through the cave before she appeared. Her eyes shone like stars on a clear summer night, her lip curled and frothing foam dripped to the floor. 'Rush home, man-boy. A storm approaches. I have much to tell you tomorrow.'

A storm? Much to tell me?

'Tell me now, please. Did you find a place?'

'Tomorrow, Cameronduncanmason. Home quickly!'

I rushed out of the cave to my bike and pedalled home faster than I ever had.

eleven

As soon as I walked in the back door, I wished I'd stayed with Dracofir and her drag-egg.

'Where on earth have you been, Cameron?' Hands on hips, right index finger and right foot tapping in time, Mum was about to transform.

'With a friend.'

'Good on you, mate. I knew you'd make friends.' Dad slapped my shoulder and continued back to the shop, crunching an apple.

'Who's your friend, Cam?' asked Justin,

smiling between forkfuls of steaming pasta. If he knew I'd had his computer game for two days he wouldn't be smiling.

'Yes, who is this friend, Cam?' Mum's finger and foot were still tapping. The squiggly purple vein in her forehead had joined the band.

'Someone I met at the lake last week.'

'So you're neglecting your jobs for someone you have just met.' She was starting to swell. 'I don't understand what is going on with you. You either totally ignore your jobs or rush around at some ungodly hour of the day disturbing everyone's sleep.'

'Mum, I —'

'Don't interrupt, Cam. You're a member of this family and have responsibilities. I just wish you could be more like Justin.' I looked at Justin. He rolled his eyes and fidgeted with his fork.

'But I'm not.' I kept my words flat and even. 'I'm me and I'm okay. I'm a good friend and I can keep a promise. I care about my friends and I don't care how they look or where they live. My friend is better to me than you are!'

Her face instantly changed from cream to purple and inflated like a balloon. The throbbing vein picked up a beat and her neck bulged over her neatly ironed white collar. Warning — marauding puffer fish ...

'Cameron, what has got into you? You have become so rude since we moved here.'

'And you have become a ... a ... grump!'

'That is it, young man, you're grounded!'

'You can't! I have to go back tomorrow. I promised.'

'Promised? You promised you'd help your father. You promised you'd do your jobs. You don't know what a promise is. Go to you room!'

I resisted the urge to throw my backpack full of books and rubbish in her face. I stormed down the hall, pausing before I slammed the door.

'That was a bit rough, Mum.' I could hear Justin going a round with the puffer fish in my defence. Funny how Justin and I could be throwing serious punches at each other one minute and sticking up for each other the next. Dad says that's what being a brother is all about. I don't know what the story is, I just wish I didn't feel so bad about him. He's a lot of fun really; it's just that he is so good at sport and I'm not.

I didn't want to hear any more. I slammed the door, swiped at the toilet paper divider and flopped onto my bed, too angry for tears.

Grounded! I couldn't be grounded. Dracofir and her drag-egg needed me. Dracofir had been half right — a storm had dumped on me, but she'd been half wrong — I wouldn't be egg-sitting for her tomorrow.

After what seemed like an hour, but was probably only a minute, there was a soft knock at the door.

'Cam, can I come in?' Dad held out a bowl of pasta. Chunky Chunks sauce slopped around the rim of the bowl. 'Thought you might be hungry.'

'I'm not.' I lay on my bed, staring at the ceiling.

'Come on, mate, I made this.'

'Boiled the water and opened the jar, you mean.' My stomach rumbled. Pasta with tomato sauce was my favourite. I sat up and took the bowl from Dad, scooping up a forkful of steaming spaghetti.

'Careful not to spill it. The puffer fish hasn't settled yet.' I nearly spat Chunky Chunks pasta across the room. How come suddenly everyone could read my mind? Dad chuckled. 'Don't look so stunned. I heard you muttering to yourself in the shop last week.' Dad smiled and patted my shoulder. 'You're right, you know.'

'Does her head kind of swell when she yells at you, Dad?'

'Yeah, and that vein in her neck bulges and thumps too.' Dad looked around my room and toed the disturbed toilet paper with his worn boot. 'Still there?'

'Until I promise to be tidy, so I guess it's there for a while.'

'Cam, tell me about your friend.'

'She's pretty cool, Dad. She lives near the lake. I've been helping her out a bit.'

'This is the old lady whose home'll be knocked down for the new tourist resort.'

'Yeah, that's her.' I made sure I spoke slowly,

terrified I would slip up and mention dragons, caves or drag-eggs.

'How well do you know her, Cam?'

'Well enough. She's from overseas, and her mate — partner — is in New Zealand on … business. She lives alone.'

'Funny set-up. Has she got kids? Anyone to help her?'

'She's pretty self-sufficient. Her young — child — died when it was ha– born.'

'That's awful, mate.'

'Yeah, she's still weird about it.'

'Is she kind, Cam? I mean, she doesn't work you too hard, does she?'

'Relax, Dad. She can be moody — you know, happy one minute and the next all grumpy and growly, but she's just worried about her egg.' Ooops … that slipped through.

'Her *egg*?'

'Yeah … she … breeds ducks and chooks and enters them in the Wilton show. Her prizewinning Rhode Island Red is sitting on eight eggs. Should hatch any day now.' I had no idea where this stuff came from, but it worked. Dad listened, nodded at all the right times, and looked sincere. Maybe I could reverse the grounding ... as long as I kept track of my fibs.

'What's her name?'

'Dra ... Mrs Dracofir.'

'Funny name!'

'It's European, Dad. She probably thinks Mason is funny too.'

'Point taken. Tell me what you do for her?'

'Tidy up, watch the hens and ducks — there's been a Jack Russell hanging around. They love to kill chooks.' All this lying was starting to worry me, especially as I was developing a bit of a talent for it. I hoped it didn't count as a bad thing when you were doing it for a good reason. Time for some truth. 'She forgave me when I made a big mistake and helped me see things differently. She's been really good to me, Dad. She trusts me.'

'We trust you too, mate, and we need your help too. Your mother is furious. You were so late home tonight, and you didn't do your jobs.'

'But I've done them every day until now, and

I was going to do them tonight. I just couldn't leave any earlier. Until today I've done all my jobs and still helped Mrs Dracofir. Mum is just cranky because I start early and she doesn't get to sleep-in. When did you last have a sleep-in, Dad?'

'That's not the point, Cam.'

'I know, but Mrs Dracofir needs my help and I know I can help her and do my jobs as well. It won't be for much longer, honest Dad.' I took another mouthful of pasta. Dad stared at his hands. 'Dad, Mum can't ground me. Mrs Dracofir needs to look for a new home. She needs someone to look after her ... eggs. Please, Dad.'

'Lot of fuss about a chook and some eggs, I reckon.' Dad smiled. 'Well, I have to say, mate, I'm proud of you. Helping a friend, especially a friend in trouble, is what life is all about.' He patted my knee. His mouth made a weird twisted grin. Dad isn't very huggy or lovey, so a pat on the knee was about as close to a hug and an 'I love you' as he would ever get. Come to think of it, I can't ever remember him telling me he was proud of me. My throat went all tight.

'I have to say, your Mum and I have noticed changes in you since you've been helping Mrs …'

'Dracofir, Dad, Mrs Dracofir. Mum! She doesn't notice anything I do, unless it's something wrong.'

'Well she has. Tonight doesn't count. She was worried about you and it came out as anger. We can both see you're happier and the spring is back in your step. You even smile a bit these days. All we ask is that your remember you have responsibilities at home as well. You have to learn to balance the two — and stop vacuuming at seven in the morning!'

'I'll try, Dad, but it's hard when she's such a — a — puffer fish all the time.' I couldn't look Dad in the eye. I knew I was close to pushing it too far.

'Its damn hard when she's so cranky, you're right, but try to be patient, mate. She misses Beldare, she's worried about you boys and she's worried about the shop. Maybe we'll have better news after the accountant's visit this afternoon.' He scratched his head and frowned. 'Tell you what, if the books are better, we'll have a week at Seal Point at Easter.'

'That would be the best!' I threw my arms around Dad's neck and hugged him tight. For someone who doesn't like hugs, he sure hugs back hard.

Happy as I was, I now faced another problem. Did I cut my losses, accept the grounding and the week at Seal Point or did I risk my dream holiday and push for the grounding to be lifted? I eased my grip on Dad and leaned back on my pillow.

'Dad, can I trade the week at Seal Point?'

'Crikey, mate, what for?' Dad sat bolt upright.

'For my grounding to be lifted.'

Dad's eyes became all cloudy and wet. 'Are you sure? Seal Point is pretty important to you.'

'I know, Dad, but Dracofir needs me and that is more important.'

'*Mrs* Dracofir, Cam; keep your manners about you.' Dad's rainy eyes became stern for a moment. 'Is it worth missing out on the beach?'

'Definitely — please, Dad.'

Dad jumped to his feet and smoothed the creases out of his trousers. 'I'll talk to your mum. Give me a few minutes, then bring your bowl to the kitchen.'

• • •

'And, Cam, no temper tantrums when Justin leaves tomorrow.'

'I promise, Mum.'

'And you must finish your jobs before you leave in the morning, and be back by six, no excuses.'

'Absolutely, Mum.'

Dad stood near the shop door while I apologised. He must have laid down the law before I arrived, because Mum looked all dopey-eyed and round-shouldered, just like Bunty used to do after I'd growled at her.

Dad stepped forward to stand beside Mum.

'Perhaps you could ask Mrs Dracofir for dinner, Cam. We'd like to meet her.' Mum fidgeted with her thumbs as she spoke.

Could be tricky. No way could I imagine Mum coping with a fire-breathing, smelly-breathed reptile as a dinner guest. 'I'll ask her, Mum, but she doesn't like going out at night.'

'All settled, Cam. You can go back to the lake tomorrow morning after you've finished your jobs.' Dad grinned and headed back to the shop. 'Better relieve Justin before he eats all the chocolate frogs.'

twelve

Mum leaned into the O'Flahertys' Range Rover and planted pink kisses on Justin's cheek. He rolled his eyes at me and waved over her shoulder.

'Have a great time, Jus,' I called. I meant it, too. I had too much to do in Wilton to worry about Seal Point.

Mum ran backwards from the car to stand with me, one hand around my shoulder, the other waving goodbye as the Range Rover crunched down the drive and into the street. We must have looked like a TV family — all smiling and lovey. Maybe we could be, if I tried harder.

'What are you up to this morning, Cam?' she asked, her hand still resting on my shoulder.

'My jobs, like you asked. Then I'll help Dad restock the icy poles and chips.'

'What about Mrs Dracofir?'

'I'd like to visit her after I'm finished, if I can.' I couldn't believe how polite I sounded. I just hoped it worked.

'You can see her now if you like.'

'What?' I screeched. So much for politeness.

Mum smiled and ruffled my hair. 'I'll help your father if you do the dinner dishes tonight.'

What had Dad said to her?

'Are you sure?' I wasn't taking any chances.

'Go on!' She gave me a little push towards the back door and laughed.

I repacked my backpack, pedalled to the lake in record time and tiptoed through the slime to Dracofir's cave. My chest felt like it would burst. I couldn't wait to tell her I'd compared her with an old woman, and her drag-egg to a hen's egg — not just any egg though — a prize-winning Rhode Island Red egg.

Dracofir had been so excited when she'd returned last night. The whole cave warmed with her joy. Her news must be incredible. I couldn't wait for her to tell me.

As soon as I crawled through the cave entrance I knew something wasn't right. It felt different; the air was biting cold. The light shining through the Eye of the Sky had changed from warm gold to harsh red, and the floor no longer sparkled.

'Dracofir!' I called, my voice quiet and quaky. My stomach filled with sharp, pointy ice which spread to my arms and legs. Goose bumps followed the icy flow. I dropped the backpack at my feet.

'Dracofir, where are you?' This time I yelled. My voice bounced from wall to wall, roof to floor.

'Quiet, Cameronduncanmason,' her voice barely a whisper. Where was she? 'I'm here.'

My stomach flipped. I clenched my sand-shoes with strong toes to stop myself falling. In the time I had been visiting Dracofir I'd never seen her in her nest and I'd never seen her look so sad.

Dracofir lay in the middle of the nest, wrapped around the drag-egg like a scarf, shoulders hunched and head low. She sang softly and swayed her head.

'Has it hatched?' I whispered.

She lifted her head and looked at me with tear-filled eyes. My heart chased itself around my chest. 'Dracofir, what is it? What happened?'

She beckoned me forward with her pointed tail. Her look told me to tread with care. I threw my arms out like a tightrope walker and stepped into the nest. I wobbled my way over the wall, into the silver layer, and took a step to the nest's third circle.

'Stop there,' commanded Dracofir in a hard whisper.

I steadied myself and watched as Dracofir uncurled her tail, bit by bit, to reveal her drag-egg.

All the colours of the drag-egg had joined together to make one glittering colour — the brightest, richest gold I'd ever seen. Its sunny glow warmed my face and body.

'Come a little closer, Cameronduncanmason … Carefully!' she added before I had lifted my foot. She didn't look at me.

Thoughts flapped around my brain like trapped butterflies. If the drag-egg was hatching, why was Dracofir so sad? Surely a hatching should be celebrated?

'What's wrong? Is the dragling all right?' My mind raced. Dracofir had explained when I egg-sat that the nest must not be disturbed or the dragling would die. I'd stomped all over the place when I first found the cave.

'Dracofir, is it something I've done?' I whispered.

She ignored my question and moved her tail a little more to reveal the dragling. 'Look!'

The dragling craned its neck over the edge of the cracked drag-egg like an inquisitive tortoise. From what I could see it was a miniature version of Dracofir, only it was a different colour. Its scales weren't rainbow-coloured like its mother's, but transparent. It looked spectacular.

With every snuffly breath, the dragling's

body filled with colour, colour that charged through its body like a rainbow and disappeared when it reached its nose and tail. A breath caught in the dragling's throat, causing small fireworks of red, purple, silver and gold to dart around inside its body. I stepped forward for a better view of the changing colours.

'It's so beautiful,' I whispered, my throat tightening.

'Look at him well, Cameronduncanmason, for he will not live much longer.'

'No, Dracofir! He will. He's so strong …' With a flick of her tail, Dracofir revealed the threat to her dragling. My voice trailed away. A piece of eggshell, as thick as my thumb and as big as my school folder, hung over the dragling's outstretched neck.

'Grab it, Dracofir!' I yelled, pointing. 'Push the dragling back into the shell! If that falls it'll kill him!'

Dracofir shook her head. A tear as blue as the sky rolled down her face.

'Dracofir, please. You have to!' My chest

burnt with anger. 'Dracofir, snap out of it!' I yelled, just like Mum yells at me when I sulk. 'Save your dragling!'

'I cannot do a thing, Cameronduncanmason.' Her voice, dripping with sorrow, was like water to my hot anger. I dropped to the floor, ignoring the sharp pieces of pink plastic and glass that jabbed my thighs and bottom.

'Why, Dracofir? Why can't you save him?'

'Cameronduncanmason, people have rules, do they not? Rules for school, rules for traffic, rules for living?'

'Dracofir, what does —?'

'Do you have rules?' She shot me a look that said I'd better answer.

'Yes.' I stared at the dragling and the hanging drag-egg shell.

'Well Cameronduncanmason, dragons too live by rules. Strict rules. Rules that keep us safe and rules that stop us hurting each other. Rules about flying and rules about magic. We have rules to prevent us eating people and rules about the ownership of our treasure. We even have rules governing dragon secrets. Our rules are strict, and punishment is swift.'

'So are you telling me that your dragling will die because I know too much about you?'

'Goodness no, man-boy, though I have bent a few rules this week. No, I am saying there are strict rules that govern the hatching of drag-eggs and that dragons are banned from interfering. We must let nature run its course.'

'Who will know if you help him? It's not like there are any dragons here who will know.'

'Remember our nine senses? Remember, man-boy, other dragons can see and feel me as I can see and feel them. It will be known if I break the rules.'

'But, Dracofir, if the drag-egg shell falls —'

'The shell is heavy and sharper than a razor. If it falls my dragling will die in the same way as my last — beheaded.' Dracofir's lower jaw quivered and another tear, this one yellow, rolled down her face.

I hugged my knees to my chest. I didn't want

to hear any more, nor did I want to see the dragling die, but I couldn't leave Dracofir, not now. I hung my head.

Maybe if I concentrated really hard, I could 'persuade' the dragling to pull its head inside the shell. Dracofir could read my thoughts; why couldn't the dragling? I lifted my head and stared at the dragling, rocking in time to the song Dracofir breathed to him.

Something sharp stabbed my bottom, but I didn't care. It didn't hurt as much as seeing the pain in Dracofir's eyes and knowing the beautiful little creature would die.

My brain felt like wet tissue paper.

'If only I ...' I muttered to my knees.

I leapt to my feet. 'Dracofir. That's it!'

'Man-boy! Settle down. Do not rush my dragling's death.' Dracofir snorted and a puff of stinky smoke settled around me.

'He doesn't have to die! I know how to save the dragling.'

'Sssit down at once sss or leave the cave, Cameronsduncanmasssson.'

'You can hiss all you like, Dracofir, but you have to listen to me.' I hoped she wouldn't risk rushing her dragling's death just to shut me up. She huffed another cloud of smoke.

'It is useless, man-boy.'

'It's not. I can move the eggshell.' I folded my arms over my chest.

Dracofir snorted. 'That is your solution?'

'Got a better one?' She shook her head. 'Then let me try, please.'

'It is forbidden.'

'Forbidden for anyone to help or just dragons?'

Dracofir lowered her head to her paws. 'There are no records of humans ever witnessing a hatching and the DDC rules make no mention of human intervention …'

'So why can't I help?'

'Because, Cameronduncanmason, we cannot interfere with nature!' A tiny spark glimmered in her eye.

'Dracofir, say you found a tiny chick fallen from its nest. Would you fly it up to its nest or leave it for the cats?' I was on shaky ground here. I only guessed Dracofir would help.

'Save it, of course,' she huffed.

'And if I knocked myself out in that stinky drain and fell face-down into the slush, would you leave me to drown or pull me to safety?'

'I would help you, of course, Cameronduncanmason. We are friends.'

'Exactly! So why can't I help you and your dragling? You said there are no rules about humans at dragling hatchings. So let me try. If it works, your dragling will live, and if it doesn't — well, nothing has changed.'

Dracofir looked from me to her dragling and back to me. Rainbow-coloured saliva dripped from her mouth and splashed at her feet.

The dragling stared at his mother, while above his head the eggshell hung still and silent. Dracofir sighed. The dragling leaned closer to her and bumped the shell. The hanging shell quivered, dropped a little, and bounced in the air like a bungee jumper.

I crossed my fingers and tried again. 'Please, Dracofir. Please. Let me help.'

'Man-boy, I should tell you one thing. The slightest cut from the drag-shell is fatal to you humans.'

Time to withdraw my offer of help. I opened my mouth to tell Dracofir when the dragling squeaked. His gaze shifted from his mother to me, his eyes misty like Lake Warrong in the rain. I remembered the dragon senses and knew he could read my thoughts and sense my fear. Somehow I could read and feel his. Warmth filled my chest, my mind whirred and my face burned. I felt confused, frightened, calm and angry. But what were my feelings and what were the dragling's? Slowly one thought bobbed to the top of my brain. I had to help.

The silence of the cave pressed heavily on my shoulders. Without breaking the quiet, Dracofir's voice filled my head — not my ears, just as it had when she showed me the world and all the damage people had done.

'Cameronduncanmason, no one, and

certainly no human, has ever offered me such a gift. I accept. Make haste before I change my mind.'

The courage that had gathered in my chest and charged out of my mouth only minutes ago dried up. The drag-egg shell cast its bleak shadow across the dragling's neck.

Could I really save the dragling?

'Mind where you step, Cameronduncanmason,' warned Dracofir, looking back over her body to where I stood. 'Look out for that goblinblood orb! And don't slip on those dried fairy wings!'

'Shut up!' I hissed. 'Dracofir, I haven't taken a step yet, and I won't if you keep that up.' I shot her my best 'Mum' dirty look — the one she does before a puffer-fish attack.

'Sorry, man-boy.' Dracofir lowered her eyes. 'Continue.'

I clenched and unclenched my clammy hands, wiped them down my T-shirt and took a deep breath. Cold sweat snaked down the back of my neck and knees. I knew a stumble, trip or bump would send the drag-egg shell falling like an axe to sever the dragling's neck. Another breath, so deep I could feel it in my toes, and I shuffled forward.

The base of the nest crunched and squeaked as I stepped from the pink layer into the yellow. Dracofir exhaled noisily. Her warm breath wrapped around me like a smelly old blanket.

So far so good — no bumps or shakes.

There were no plastic or glass pieces to trip me up in the yellow circle, so, confident, I went forward. Two steps and I lost my balance. I gave a Homer Simpson 'Doh' and threw my arms out like a trapeze artist.

'CARE—' Dracofir covered her huge eyes with a glittering foreleg.

I wobbled on tiptoes, leaning so far forward my forehead brushed against a gritty chunk of old carpet. Somehow I regained my balance without falling and without shaking the drag-egg. It was harder to steady my chugging heart. I waited, eyes closed, expecting to hear Dracofir cry out as the dragling died.

Once again silence settled over the cave.

'I'm sorry, I panicked,' whispered Dracofir. 'The dragling is fine. Continue, Cameronduncanmason.'

I wiped my palms and prepared to move forward.

'But before you move, may I just say, it would pay to treat the bumps in the nest floor with great care, as they are hollow.' Her eyes avoided mine.

'Now you tell me,' I muttered. Sweat prickled my scalp and trickled down my face. My heart pounded against my ribs. At this rate I'd have a heart attack before I reached my next birthday.

With outstretched arms I continued forward, avoiding the bumps and hollows in the nest floor. A few wobbly steps and I reached Dracofir. My next challenge was to find a path around her body.

'Climb over my tail, Cameronduncanmason. It is the quickest and easiest way.'

It was one thing to touch her cheek, but climbing over her body was a whole different story. I reached out and stroked her tail. Her scales were warm and smooth under my fingertips. I could barely feel where one glittering scale finished and the next began.

'Remember, man-boy, dragons are able to smell and taste danger, and when we do, we toughen our scales to make them impenetrable. Now climb over. This is taking too much time, by far.'

I wedged my hands between the jagged spikes that flowed the length of her spine and heaved myself up, like I do when I climb out of the deep end of the pool. I jammed my feet between the spikes.

Dracofir groaned and grunted. 'Mind where you poke those shoes, Cameronduncanmason.'

I stood as high as the roof of a four-wheel-drive. Below me I could see the entire egg, the dragling and the piece of skin holding the dangling shell. It was as thick as a shoelace and stretched tight. Parts of it were starting to fray. The slightest bump would snap the thread.

'How will I get down?' Jumping was out of the question and if I slid down I would shake the nest. I felt a tap on my shoulder and turned to see the tip of Dracofir's tail pointed at me.

'Hold this.'

I rubbed my sweaty hands on my shorts and grabbed on.

'Not too tight,' said Dracofir with a sharp breath.

'Don't be a sook!'

She lifted her tail high into the air, held it steady for a moment, then lowered me to her dragling.

Rubies and diamonds squealed under my feet as I stepped into the centre of the nest, careful not to stand between the two dragons and block their dragon think-talk.

The drag-egg was as high as my chest and wider than my arm-span. The shell, thicker than my thumb, pulsed with spectacular bubbles of gold, pink and brown. The lines had disappeared, allowing all the colours to blend.

The dragling, too, was a mass of life and colour. Because he was transparent, I could see his blood pulse through his body, not red like mine, but a sparkling rainbow. I could see his scales, the spikes that travelled the length of his spine, his long talons — not black like Dracofir's, but clear, and the cream wings wrapped tightly on his back.

'You are beautiful,' I smiled.

'There will be time for that later, Cameron-duncanmason. Make haste.'

And make haste I did. Perhaps it was the excitement of being so close to a baby dragon, or the thrill of the magic before me — whatever it was, I didn't wait an extra second to plan my move. I grabbed the hanging shell between my fingers and thumbs, careful not to let the sparkling edges too close to my palms.

I immediately regretted my rush. Between my sweaty and slippery fingers, the shell slipped. It was too late to let go and try again or even change my grip. The thread had snapped. I held the eggshell's weight, and the life of the dragling, in my hands.

thirteen

The shell slipped towards the dragling's neck.

I froze. If I gripped the shell tighter I would cut myself on the sharp edges and die, and if I dropped the shell, the dragling would die. It was a choice between death and death. My knees wobbled and buckled.

Dracofir moaned.

I grunted and puffed. I was losing the battle to hold the load.

The image of a discus thrower at the

Olympics filled my mind. I could see him spinning around and tossing the discus. It sliced through the air and landed with a bump on the green turf. I was good at discus. It was the only thing I liked about Little Aths — that and shot-put, but why was I thinking about that when either the dragling or I was about to die?

I laughed out loud. That was it! I ground my teeth together and took a long breath. Squinting, I scanned the cave for a gap. A half-cry, half-grunt escaped from my throat as I flung the drag-shell over Dracofir's tail towards the cave wall.

The force of the throw knocked me off my feet. I landed face-down in the sparkling jewels. I rolled onto my back and lay there, too sore and too scared to lift my head to see if the dragling had survived.

My head hurt. I touched it and felt thick sweat — at least, I thought it was sweat. I stared at my hand. Bright blood covered my grimy fingers and dripped onto my palm. Icy panic charged through my body. I sat up and whimpered, 'Dracofir.'

'You nearly sliced off my tail, Cameron-duncanmason.' Dracofir studied her tail and snorted pink smoke. She shook herself, uncurled her body and stretched.

'I'm about to die and you're worried about your stupid tail!' Tears filled my eyes. I didn't want to die. I'd made a friend — it might be a female dragon, but it was still a friend. Mum was really trying and Dad was listening to me again. I wondered how much time I had left. My head throbbed. Could that be the first sign of drag-shell poisoning?

'You have gashed your head on the Dwarf's Diamond, man-boy.'

To my left lay a crystal-clear diamond, shaped like a small man, and it was splattered with blood.

'So I'm not going to die?' My legs and arms turned into jelly. I sniffed and laughed at once.

Dracofir did the foamy, snarly, grinny thing. She lifted her front leg and touched my forehead with a long black talon. A burning white pain filled my head, then nothing. 'You will not die for a long time yet, my friend.'

I poked my forehead with a shaky finger — no pain, no blood, no cut, not even a scratch. 'How'd you do that?'

Ignoring my question she brushed my cheek with her talon and rested her claw upon my shoulder.

'Thank you, Cameronduncanmason. Thank you.'

A tear rolled down my face. I looked at the dragling so Dracofir wouldn't see what a cry-baby I was.

The dragling paid no attention to me or to his mother. He was arching his neck, twisting his head from side to side and bumping the rest of the drag-egg shell until it tipped forward. He crawled out onto the sparkling jewels.

'Cameronduncanmason, let me introduce my first male dragling. The first male hatched in my family for one hundred years. His name will be Dracocam.'

'Dracocam. It's a good name. It's kind of

strong. Does it mean anything special?'

'Indeed it does. "Draco" signifies my ancient dragon family lines stretching back to Earth's early days. "Cam" signifies our friendship, your help and your courage. I have named my dragling after you, for you are my friend. Dracocam. It is a good name. A strong name. A gentle name. It is like you, Cameronduncanmason.'

Just when my eyes had cleared they misted again. 'But Dracofir, I'm not strong or good. And I haven't been a good friend. Don't you remember, I tried to …'

'It matters not. You returned to my cave. Despite my lack of manners, you gave up what you desired the most, for my sake, and you helped when all seemed hopeless. That is true friendship, Cameronduncanmason. We do not always get it right, but when we do, it is the purest magic.' Dracofir's lips twisted. She grasped me with both her front claws and pressed me to her chest. I could hear her heart thud and the blood swoosh in her chest. Tears chased each other down my face.

'No one has ever said —'

'Nor to me. Perhaps both of us had best learn to forgive and to trust.' She released her grip and wiped my tears with the same talon that healed my bleeding head. She reached behind me and scooped up her dragling, bringing him into the small space between us. 'Now forgive my rudeness once again, Cameronduncanmason, but there are rituals I must perform with my son, Dracocam. Rituals which none, not even another dragon, may see. Go home now. Your parents are waiting. They have a surprise for you.'

I stroked Dracocam's flank before hopping and jumping across the nest surface to the cave entrance. It didn't matter what I kicked or bumped. It didn't matter if I fell and destroyed the nest, scattering twigs, plastic, jewels and branches across the cave — the dragling had hatched.

Before I crouched down to crawl through the tunnel, I turned to look back at the nest. Once again the cave floor sparkled and gleamed. Golden light streamed through the Eye of the Sky, replacing the harsh red light. I breathed deeply. The taste of freshly-cut grass and sun-warmed hay had replaced the icy air. Each breath filled my body with warmth and happiness.

'Dracofir, can I return tomorrow?'

'Please do, Cameronduncanmason. I have not yet shared my good news with you.'

fourteen

I had five near misses on the way home. I had to wrench my handlebars hard to the left and only just missed a chugging bulldodozer. Men wearing safety hats and bright orange reflector vests yelled and shook their fists at me. I rode into the gutter twice trying to weave out of their way. I warped my wheel a little, but didn't hit any of the waving men.

My next near accident involved a power-pole — if I hadn't hit the brakes I would have ridden straight into that, and then there was the telephone box. I'm sure the glass already had a crack in it.

It was impossible to concentrate. I had just seen, no — helped, a baby dragon hatch.

The sky was bluer and the grass greener but my road sense was shocking! Though I did notice that the wattle birds and magpies were quiet for a change.

I rubbed my jaw with one hand and steered with the other. No wonder my face ached. I was grinning like a Tattslotto winner, only my prize was better. I had a dragling named after me. Me! Cam Mason! Maybe I wasn't a good catch or a top footy player, but I was a great drag-egg shell thrower!

I skidded to a halt by the back door, jumped off my bike and burst into the kitchen. I froze midstep. Mum and Dad sat at the table, talking. They stopped and stared at me. What now? I glanced at my watch. Four-thirty pm. I wasn't late.

The cheesy grin and warmth in my stomach slid away like melting snow.

'Hi,' I muttered.

'Cam! Glad you're back. We've been waiting for you.' Dad smiled. It must be bad if he was doing all the talking. I stared at my feet.

'Don't stand there — go get changed,' said Mum. At least I think it was Mum — it looked like her, but her voice was all sunny and breezy.

My heart sank into the mud of my fears. Mum had talked Dad into selling me off or having me adopted. She wanted me in clean clothes so I looked my best. They'd get rid of me quicker if I looked clean and tidy. I couldn't blame her really. I'd been pretty revolting since we moved to Wilton. My feet twitched. I wanted to run back to Dracofir and beg her to let me live with her and Dracocam forever. She'd said my parents had a surprise for me, not a shock.

'Get changed for what?'

'Thought the three of us should see that new Bruce Willis film,' said Dad.

'And have dinner out, too. Your choice,' added Mum with a smile — a smile that made her eyes twinkle.

'What?' A film and dinner? All three of us? I

couldn't remember the last time Mum and Dad had taken me out and I couldn't imagine them shutting the shop for the night. This was seriously weird.

'Cam, you are filthy!' Mum leaned back in the chair and looked me over. 'Covered in Mrs Dracofir's chook poo, by the look of you.'

I looked down. Filthy? Disgustingly! Even I thought I looked a disgrace. I'd slipped, skidded and slid through the drain, and in my excitement had forgotten to change my clothes. I swallowed. Here it comes …

'Lucky you're on laundry duty for a bit longer, I'd say.' Dad grinned.

'Yes, I'm glad I don't have to deal with those,' said Mum, pointing at my clothes. 'Go on, in the shower.'

No puffer-fish attack? No lecture? Maybe Dracofir had fried their brains with some dragon magic or maybe part of her magic was the ability to perform personality make-overs. Or maybe an alien had kidnapped my parents — perhaps that was the surprise!

I weaved around the kitchen table and headed for the bathroom. Would my real parents be waiting in a cloud of Dracofir's smelly smoke when I returned?

'Cam,' said Mum. Here it comes! 'Did the eggs hatch?'

My brighter-than-sunshine, split-your-face grin returned. I spun to face her, hands beating the air like Mr Androtious, the market greengrocer. 'Sure did. The eggshell got stuck. Looked like it'd kill the chick. It was tough going for a bit, but I helped. I saved the dra … chicken.' Excitement filled my chest to bursting point. I had to talk about it.

'Fantastic!' Mum smiled that twinkly smile again.

'Congratulations, mate,' said Dad. 'Now hurry up. The film starts at five-thirty.'

'But Dad — well — what about the shop? You can't just close it.'

'Mrs Johnston is working for us. You've spent so much time with Mrs Dracofir today I haven't told you the good news. The accountant said the books are much better than we expected. We can afford to hire help and that means life will become a little easier.' Dad looked around, then whispered, 'Good old Pucker, eh?'

Dad and I giggled.

'Cam.' The smile faded from Mum's face and she studied the scuffed pine table. 'I'm proud of you — how you've tried to keep up with your jobs and help Mrs Dracofir. She must be pretty special if you're willing to give up a holiday at Seal Point for her.' Mum looked up. Her eyes were filled with tears. 'I'm sorry. The move has been hard and we — well, I've been tough on you.' I couldn't make out the feelings that crossed her face, but I knew she was sorry.

'It's getting better though, isn't it?' I grinned and ran down the hall to the bathroom. I didn't know what else to say. I'd never seen Mum cry before, and I didn't want to see it today.

fifteen

'Cam, if you're making toast, pop a slice in for me, please.' The newspaper rustled as Mum turned the page.

'I'm still full from the Chinese food last night, but I'll make you some.'

'You and your father love those prawns. I don't know how you eat them.' Mum wrinkled her nose and shuddered.

'You're missing out, Mum!' I grinned. 'The film was good too.'

'Had a strange effect on your dad. Should have seen him shaving — he tried the one-liners in the mirror and used his razor as the gun. Bruce Willis he ain't!' She shook her head and giggled, making a tinkling sound in her throat. I hadn't heard that noise since we came to Wilton.

'You had fun, Mum?'

She placed her steaming mug of tea on the coaster and perched on the edge of her chair. 'It was a lovely night, Cam. We'll do it again when Justin returns from Seal Point.' She sipped her tea. 'Cam, ask Mrs Dracofir for dinner tonight. We'd like to meet her. Besides, she must be so lonely and scared with the development starting today.'

'Today?' I screeched like a cockatoo. I'm sure my hair stood up like a cocky's crest too.

'Didn't you see the bulldozers on your way home from the lake yesterday? We could hear the rumbling from here. Made the glass bottles chink in the drink refrigerator!'

The bulldozers! Men in safety hats and reflector vests! What an idiot. I had been so excited after helping Dracocam hatch I hadn't paid attention. The men screamed and waved at me because I was riding through the construction site. No wonder the magpies and wattle birds were quiet and, come to think of it, none of the water birds — ducks, swamp hens, coots or swans — were puddling in the shallows of the lake when I rode past. My heart dropped like the big dipper.

'I have to go.'

'Cam, what is it?'

'Dracofir … I have to help her. She needs me.' I was on my feet and running before I'd finished speaking.

'Cam, the dishes,' called Mum behind me.

• • •

I rounded the Birre Road corner and turned into Lake Drive. Lake Warrong lay before me like a jewelled picnic blanket, sparkling and twinkling under the summer sun. Down the steep embankment, plastic orange barriers fluttered in the breeze. Scarred yellow bulldozers dozed on the green grass like sleeping giants. Men wearing hard hats scurried ant-like around the water's edge and the drain which led to Dracofir's cave. Getting through was going to be tough.

I slipped off my bike above the construction site. I hid it beneath a bottlebrush shrub and stood for a moment watching the activity below. I needed to plan. There was no way I was rushing into this one.

It was just after 8 am. Some of the workers walked around the site, consulting large maps and notebooks while others inspected bulldozers and earthmovers. Apart from the orange barrier extending to the far side of it, none of the men seemed too interested in the drain yet.

I decided the best approach was to crawl commando-style down the far embankment. It was easier thought than done. The summer sun had sucked all the moisture from the grass, and stubble grabbed at my face, arms and legs, biting like a fizzed kitten. And if the grass wasn't painful enough, the bindi-eyes killed! No wonder they punctured bike tyres. If there's ever another war, I reckon the army should farm bindi-eye patches and use them instead of minefields.

When the first bindi-eye stabbed my palm, I bit my lip, buried my face in my arm and pulled out the thorn without making a sound. I wasn't as brave when the next one pierced my knee. I screamed.

I pressed myself flat into the grass, listened and waited to be found, but nothing happened so I pulled out the thorn and crawled on. By the time I reached the drain's opening, I looked like something out of a jungle war.

I stood rigid for a moment and watched. Two men holding a map between them approached the drain, looked at it and then returned to the shed. Once they'd disappeared, I ducked into the drain.

Actually, I slid and slipped into the drain, and landed with a squelch, face-down in the filth. I gagged at the smell and staggered to my feet, shaking my arms and legs, trying to dislodge the muck that covered me. Voices outside the drain grew louder so I abandoned my careful approach and ran as best I could.

Once I reached the dry path to Dracofir's

cave, I wanted to shout and yell a warning about the development but I was frightened the workers would hear me and come to investigate. I couldn't bring myself to think about what would happen if the workers found Dracofir and Dracocam.

I dropped to my stinging knees and crawled through the tunnel.

The cave was dark and silent. The glittering floor and the nest that protected the drag-egg, were gone. No twig, jewel, chain or piece of glass lay on the floor to hint at what might have been there. Beneath my feet was smooth, pressed earth. I looked to the Eye of the Sky — gone. In its place were knotted and gnarled tree roots.

I flopped to the floor. Every muscle ached and every scratch burned. Pain filled my head and chest. I dropped my head in my hands.

'Dracofir, why didn't you say goodbye?'

'How bad you smell, Cameronduncanmason!'

I leapt to my feet and looked around. Nothing — except for two boulders, one smaller than the other, resting against the back wall. They began to twist and turn as I approached. Both changed colour from stone grey to pink to blue as they bulged and shuddered. Sparks of colour and smoke flew out of the smaller boulder. With a hiss and a rattle, the boulders became Dracofir and Dracocam.

'Not bad for a first effort, not bad at all,' said Dracofir as she nuzzled her dragling with her long snout. 'And as for you, smelly one, I thought you would know where to look by now.'

I sniffed. 'The nest, the floor — I thought you'd gone.'

'Without saying goodbye? You must think us dragons of ill-breeding.' Dracofir's lip curled and a puff of pink smoke escaped her mouth and nostrils. I had learned something. I knew a dragon smile when I saw it. 'In answer to your question, the floor and my treasures are secure, packed away. I have dealt with my nest and the Eye of the Sky as tradition dictates. All is in readiness for our departure.'

'You must hurry, Dracofir. They are here. The workers have arrived.'

'I know. I felt their preparations yesterday. It is time to leave this place, Cameronduncanmason.'

'But where will you go?'

'That is the news I did not tell you. I have found a new home, an underground cave beside an ancient spring within the Geonite Rainforest.'

'I see.' A pretty weird thing to say, but my brain went blank — all white and empty. In the short time I'd known her, I'd come to love Dracofir. I didn't think she would really leave, not now that we were friends. 'You'd better go then. They'll start those bulldozers soon.'

'It is time we left, yes.' She scooped up Dracocam and sat him on her shoulders, just above her wings. She fussed and fidgeted, adjusting the dragling and her scales until she was content. The dragling looked down at me, his deep chocolate eyes looking straight through my skin, into my soul. Warmth filled my chest.

'Goodbye, Dracocam.' I reached up and stroked his scaled head. He closed his eyes and squeaked.

'One so small cannot fly until the seventh year,' said Dracofir. 'I shall carry him to our home.'

I nodded. Fresh tears welled in my eyes and tightness stung my throat. I'd cried more this week than I had in my whole life. 'Goodbye, Dracofir. I'll miss you.' I stepped forward and hugged her, surprised again at how smooth and warm she was to touch.

'Farewell, Cameronduncanmason. Travel with care and a light heart on your life's journey.'

She arched her back and spread her wings. Sparkling glitter rained onto the cave floor.

'Goodbye, my friend.' She flapped her wings and rose to the cave roof.

'Dracofir, wait!' I called as she shrank before my eyes. I had so many questions and so much to tell her. I wanted to tell her about last night, to thank her for being my friend, for helping me. But she didn't wait. In a cloud of stinking, coloured smoke she disappeared, becoming smaller and smaller with each wing-beat until she was the size of a bee. She flapped out of the cave and out of my life.

Sorrow gathered in my toes and spread through my body, yet no fresh tear fell. The rumble of a bulldozer's engine broke my daze. I blinked and looked around the cave one last time. I stared up at the gnarled roots where the Eye of the Sky had been and walked towards the ledge where Dracofir had first stared down at me and spoken in her hissing voice. I could hear her snarling laugh and could feel her warmth. I smiled at the memories dancing in my mind.

The earth rumbled as the engine moved. Instead of glitter, a spray of dirt rained to the cave floor. It was time to leave.

'Thank you, Dracofir.' I threw my arms out wide and spun around, yelling the words into the dirt-filled air, hoping a breath of wind would carry them to her.

The throb of the engines shook the roof. Dirt fell and settled on my head, shoulders and the cave floor.

A glint of red caught my eye. Dracofir must have left a piece of her nest behind. The closer I came, the more it glittered and shone. I bent to pick it up and gasped. It was the jewel that had been caught in the cuff of my shorts the first time I'd visited the cave. It covered my entire hand from the tips of my fingers to my wrist.

'A ruby,' I murmured. Mum's engagement ring was this colour and she'd told me the name of the stone.

The rich red jewel, shaped like a teardrop, felt heavy, but not cold or sharp as I'd expected. It was warm and smooth, and as I moved it, glittering colours, like those of Dracofir's scales and Dracocam's blood, shone on my body and the cave walls. It had to be special. I had to return it to Dracofir.

'But how do I find you?' I asked, staring into the red stone on my palm.

'It will not be difficult, Cameronduncanmason.' I jumped, nearly dropping the stone, and looked around the cave, expecting another of Dracofir's tricks. But the cave was empty. When I looked into the stone, her voice continued, filling my head, though I wasn't hearing it with my ears.

'While you have the Dragon's Tear, I will be

able to find you, and you will be able to find me.' I ran around the cave, searching for her, slapping rocks and pinching boulders.

'We have left this place, Cameronduncanmason, but I leave you this gift. The Dragon's Tear is a ruby of great value, yet it must not be sold. Keep it with you always and we will be able to find each other. Look into the Dragon's Tear, Cameronduncanmason, and I will be there.'

I stared into the ruby and Dracofir stared back at me. I could hear and feel the whoosh of her wings as she cut through the sky. The roar of the wind filled my head. Dracocam peered over his mother's shoulder. Dracofir smiled her twisted, drippy smile. 'Cameronduncanmason, I thank you for your friendship which has been tested by us both, yet triumphed. Friendships among your own kind will be easier now. Believe in yourself and believe that to have a friend you need to be a friend, just as it has been with us. Until next we meet ...'

Her face began to fade into the ruby. I gripped the red stone and held it to my heart before thrusting it into my pocket. Her words had made me feel better and her gift had filled me with hope. I plodded to the cave entrance and looked around for the last time.

'Goodbye,' I whispered.

A warm, gold light filled the cave for a moment and flickered. Then the cave plunged into darkness. I crawled through the tunnel for the last time and stumbled along the dry path to the sludgy drain. Again I slipped and slid through the ankle-deep grunge. The throb of the bulldozer picked up a beat and I picked up my speed.

'How come the drain is so slimy in the middle of summer?' I muttered, struggling to stay upright. Bright sunshine flooded into the mouth of the drain, blinding me. I released my grip on the cement wall to shield my eyes and fell with a splat onto the crushed cans, rotting pigeon and mouldy paper that carpeted the drain's entrance. Something warm and rough licked my face.

'What the …?' I pushed myself up onto my knees. A black Labrador stood panting and grinning at me in a dog sort of way. I scratched him behind the ears, just like I used to scruff Bunty, and felt for a collar. From the collar's buckle dangled a large gold star with 'Rocky Franklin' engraved across it.

'Are you Tim's dog?' The dog panted, then sniffed the pigeon carcass. I heard voices outside the cave.

'Hurry up and find your mutt! We're about to rip open this drain,' said a gruff voice.

'I think he went in there.' It sounded like Tim Franklin.

I grabbed Rocky by the collar and led him through the sludge and out into the sunlight.

'Here he is, Tim.' I patted Rocky's head.

'Where the hell did you come from?' asked gruff man.

'In there.' I nodded at the drain. 'I saw Rocky bolt in and went to get him.'

'Righto. Time's money. You've got your dog so clear off home.'

Tim and I ran up the embankment, with Rocky loping along beside us. The Dragon's Tear jabbed into my thigh with every step.

'And put that dog on a lead,' yelled gruff man after us.

'Gotta get my bike and head home,' I said to Tim when we reached the top.

'Yeah, me too. What were you doing in that drain?'

'Long story.' I stared at my feet, frightened Tim would see the sorrow in my eyes. 'I lost my tennis ball.'

'Right.' Tim grabbed Rocky's collar. 'Be seeing you then.'

'Does Rocky like fetching balls and sticks and stuff?' I must have shouted because both Tim and Rocky stopped in their tracks.

'Yeah. Why?'

'Maybe we could go to the oval tomorrow and chuck some stuff for him.'

'Yeah, OK. I'll come by the shop.'

'See you then.' I turned and jogged to where I'd left my bike. I pulled it out from under the bottlebrush and pedalled home, squeezing my pocket every few pedals to make sure the Dragon's Tear was still there. Excitement rose in my chest.

I was going to hang out with Tim — maybe we'd even become friends. Friends ... Dracofir. Sadness dulled my excitement. Dracofir was gone.

I dropped my bike beside the back doorstep and walked inside, head hanging low. Mum was still in the kitchen, humming along to the radio, drying the dishes.

'Cam! That didn't take long. Here, help me finish these.' Mum tossed me a tea towel. It flopped to the floor.

I stared at the cracked lino.

'Cam, is everything all right? Is Mrs Dracofir okay?'

'She can't come for dinner, Mum.' A fat tear spilt from my left eye, rolled down my face and splashed onto the toe of my shoe. 'She left this morning. She's gone somewhere safe with her son.' More fat tears began to flow. Mum edged around the table and gripped my shoulders.

'Oh Cam, you'll see her again, I know it.'

I thrust my left hand into my pocket. The Dragon's Tear felt warm, heavy and hidden.